Sacrificing Love

A Black Hollow Story

I0546216

Cassidy K· O'Connor

Dedication

To all the hopeless romantics out there, keep your hearts open and ready for love. You never know when it will show up in your life, sometimes even with an ugly dog in tow.

To the Black Hollow Authors, thank you for recognizing how special this town is and helping us create amazing characters for the readers to fall in love with.

One

"Sarah, you've only been with Adam seven months, are you sure you're ready to marry him?" Ivy bit her lip nervously hoping she hadn't offended her cousin. "After everything with your ex, I just want to make sure the next guy that falls for you is Mr. Forever." She held the phone between her shoulder and ear.

Ivy heard her cousin chuckle softly before responding. "I know you haven't met him yet, but you have no idea how apropos your name for him is. I know you are coming next weekend for the bridal shower, how about you come a week early and spend time with us? I want my Maid of Honor and my fiancé to be friends."

Ivy studied the calendar on her laptop, deciding which meetings she could reschedule.

"I'm not sure I can get time off work."

"I know you think we live in some small podunk town but trust me we have internet and we both know you can work from pretty much anywhere."

Ivy contemplated her options for a brief second, "If you can put up with me for a whole week, then I would love to come out early. I'll pack up tonight and get out there first thing tomorrow." Ever the efficient one she already had three emails and a meeting invite open getting ready to lighten her schedule for the visit. "Do you know if the Inn allows dogs? I don't want to get a pet sitter for that long."

"Let's be honest, you don't want to be away from your new puppy for that long. Let me call the Inn and get back to you. Either way, we'll find somewhere for you and the pup to stay."

Ivy couldn't help letting out a small squeal of excitement. Sarah had told her a little about Black Hollow, and she couldn't wait to visit. "Sounds like a plan, see you tomorrow!"

Once she was alone with her thoughts again, she let doubt creep in. Her cousin was abused by her first husband for many years. She finally got away and was getting her life straight when she up and meets a guy in some town Ivy had never heard of and not even a year later they are getting married. Isn't that how most abuse cases start, the guy sweeps the girl off her feet then once she's locked in he shows his true self?

Ivy knew the only way to feel happy for her cousin on her wedding day was if she went early and did what any woman would do and stalk the hell out of him and make sure he was good enough for Sarah.

Two

As Ivy passed the sign welcoming her to Black Hollow, her eyes grew huge. Sarah had described the town but actually seeing it for the first time put her words to shame.

It was as if she had driven back in time. People strolled up and down the streets, stopping to mingle. If that wasn't unusual enough in this day and age, some of the people looked odd...some had skin thin enough it was almost translucent. Others had horns or tails sticking out of various parts of their bodies.

Sarah had warned her the town was eccentric and embraced the year-round Halloween theme, however, Ivy was not prepared for how authentic everything was. "Would you look at this place, Zeus." She glanced down at her eight-month-old puppy who sat on the passenger seat staring up at her with large brown eyes. "I can't believe my cautious, straight-laced cousin is living here."

The tiny dog whined at her. "I know, this Adam guy must be pretty amazing to get her to uproot Alex and move here." Ivy knew people thought she was crazy when she talked to the dog like he was a person. She didn't really care, she would choose him over most humans in a heartbeat.

The car's GPS had her jumping when the voice announced the next turn was coming. She pulled up to the apartment building and parked. Scooping Zeus up she locked her car and made her way to Sarah and Adam's apartment.

Ivy knocked then laughed as she heard multiple people from inside yell out, "She's here."

The door was opened by a beaming Sarah with her son Alex standing next to her. The man behind her shocked Ivy for a brief second. Sarah had warned her he had scarring from an accident when he was younger, but Ivy wasn't prepared for the sheer amount of tiny, silver lines crisscrossing every bit of exposed skin including his face.

"Hey Cuz, welcome to Black Hollow. Come in and meet Adam." The trio stood back and waved her over to the couches.

"Alex, I haven't seen you in so long, you are almost taller than me." She smiled as the boy's chest puffed up. He still wasn't close to her five feet four inches, but she knew he would like hearing the compliment.

"Can I pet your dog?" Alex reached his hand towards the animal in her arms.

"That's a dog?" Ivy ignored Adam's whispered question to Sarah.

Most people didn't appreciate Zeus's unique features. She didn't mind their poor taste. In her eyes, there was no cuter dog in the world.

"This is Zeus, he loves to be scratched on his belly." She sat on the couch, the dog immediately rolled on its back and put all four legs in the air, waiting for his belly to be scratched.

"Now it just looks like roadkill," Adam whispered loudly, Sarah elbowed his side.

"I talked to Sandy at the Inn, and he isn't comfortable with you bringing a dog. He is very particular about the guests getting a quiet, relaxing atmosphere to rest in, and he thinks Zeus will be a noisy distraction." Sarah held her hand up at the look of panic on Ivy's face. "Don't worry, though, the apartment below us is fully furnished and empty at the moment. You can stay there for the week if you'd like."

Ivy was relieved, for a brief second, she pictured having to sleep on their couch. "Sure, I'm happy to bunk anywhere." That was a stretch but isn't that the appropriate response?

"The only thing is, the previous tenant, Raveena, was practicing one of her hobbies with a friend of ours, Alizon, and they managed to damage one of the walls. We have someone coming over to fix it so it will be good as new in no time."

Ivy's eyes bulged, "That sounds like a dangerous hobby."

Sarah shrugged but didn't feel the need to elaborate.

"If you want, Alex and I can grab your bags and take them to the apartment?" Adam offered.

Ivy blanked for a second, the sight of his scars catching her off guard again. She had to admit, they did add a level of gorgeousness to him. "Um, I actually have a lot of stuff because of the bridal shower. I'll come down and help."

The group made their way downstairs to the car. Adam whistled when he opened the trunk.

"I know it looks like a lot. I wasn't sure what stores you had around here, so I decided to bring everything with me." She grabbed her backpack off the top of the pile. "Sarah, you hold Zeus and hang back, no peeking." She handed over the pet and grabbed a box. "Lead the way."

Adam handed Alex a light box and grabbed what he could. As they made their way to her temporary home, the sound of hammering reached their ears.

"Toussaint must have snuck in already to start on the wall." Sarah opened the apartment door and led the group inside.

Ivy froze a few steps inside. A large, muscular man with no shirt on and low hanging jeans was tearing down the wall that separated the living room and the bedroom. Sweat rolled down his spine, Ivy gulped at the sight.

"TOUSSAINT," Adam yelled to get his attention.

The giant spun around in surprise. "Oh hey, sorry I didn't get to this yesterday. I know you wanted it done before your cousin got here, but Saroj had me building an eight-foot-tall ice cream cone to go on the roof of his shop."

The group laughed, Ivy was lost at why that was so funny.

"Good lord Sarah, what is that thing in your arms?" Toussaint stared at Zeus with a look of disgust on his face.

Ivy immediately became defensive, "That would be my dog, Zeus." She didn't mean to sound snippy, but really the big oaf was criticizing the love of her life.

He turned and immediately looked like he regretted saying anything, "I'm sorry, I didn't see you there. I was just taken by surprise, I've never seen a... breed...quite like that."

"That's because there is no one like Zeus." Ivy shot back.

"Thank god for that," Adam whispered.

Ivy didn't think he realized how bad he was at whispering.

Toussaint glanced at the hairy creature one last time before looking back at Adam. "My apologies again. It shouldn't take me long to get this hole patched up then I'll be out of your hair." He nodded and turned back around to continue working.

Ivy was perplexed how this man was going to build an entire wall in a couple of hours. Honestly, she didn't need the wall, so she wasn't too worried about it being done. Plus, the man may have poor taste in pets, but he was a beautiful sight, so maybe she didn't mind if it took him a while to finish.

Sarah grabbed one of the boxes from Adam and set it on the kitchen table. "How about we go get lunch and get out of Toussaint's way for a while?"

Ivy glanced over to the giant who had already dismissed them. "Is there somewhere we can eat outside, so I don't have to leave Zeus here?" Ivy wasn't sure she trusted Toussaint not to accidentally step on her pup and crush him.

Sarah smiled, "Feel like fish and chips?"

Three

Ivy walked beside her cousin as they walked to the restaurant. "I thought you were crazy when you told me you were moving here, but I can see the charm of the town. Everyone craves that small town feel and you actually have it here."

"Everyone has been really accepting of Alex and I. This truly has been the best decision I've ever made." Sarah glowed with happiness.

"I'm sure the town is a nice bonus, but we both know the main attraction is that fine piece of ass walking in front of us." Ivy laughed at Sarah's shock, "Come on, admit it, he's good in bed, isn't he?"

Sarah elbowed her, "You always were a horn ball."

"That is not an answer." Ivy wasn't giving up.

Sarah leaned close and whispered, "Don't let the scars fool you, every part of that man works perfectly, and he's definitely the best I've ever had."

"Now I'm jealous, does he have a brother?" Ivy joked.

"No, but there are so many fine pieces of ass in this town I will be mad if you don't get some action while you're here." It was Ivy's turn to look surprised at her cousin's words. She wasn't usually so bold.

Ivy almost asked if the giant back in her temporary apartment was available. She resisted though, she didn't want her cousin focusing on anything except her upcoming wedding.

As they made their way toward the center of town, Ivy couldn't help but be jealous of her cousin's new home. The unusual looking townsfolk were walking around, stopping to talk to people they pass by. Some were laying in the grass eating ice cream as if they were in some Hallmark movie.

A loud shriek ahead of them caught Ivy's attention, "Oh my god, that boy has his hand up that woman's skirt." Ivy watched with confusion as the woman laughed and gently swatted the boy's hand away, then bent and kissed him quite thoroughly on the mouth.

"Oh my god, did you see that? We have to do something." Ivy's heart was racing, her instinct to protect had gone into overdrive.

Sarah grabbed her arm and pulled her back, she held her finger up, telling Ivy to wait. Sarah was laughing so hard she wasn't able to talk yet.

When she finally caught her breath, she wiped tears from her eyes before explaining. "He's a little person, I promise you he is older than both of us."

Ivy's head swung back to the couple, her cheeks reddened with embarrassment when the man turned around, and she could see he was no child.

"Arden, Kerry." Adam waved at the couple who waved back and made their way over to their group.

Ivy was mortified, she knew the man didn't know she had just accused him of being a boy, but it didn't make her feel any less guilty.

Adam gestured towards her. "Hey guys, this is Sarah's Cousin, Ivy. She came in early for the wedding."

Kerry waved, "Nice to meet you, I think the whole town is buzzing with wedding excitement."

Ivy leaned back as the man across from her, leaned in close to Zeus. "Well, would you look at that, if I didn't know better I'd swear that's a Cwn Annwn."

"That's a new one sweetie, say it again." Kerry stared intently at the man's lips.

"The spelling is ridiculous but easy to pronounce, just say coon anoon."

Kerry repeated it a couple of times. "I've been trying to learn some of his native language. I've found it doesn't sound as good without the accent."

Ivy thought their interaction was sweet. She wasn't sure though if she should be offended by whatever he just called her dog. She leaned over and whispered to Sarah, "Help me remember the words, I need to Google what he said and see if he was insulting Zeus."

Alex pulled on Sarah's hand. "Mommy, I'm hungry, can we go now?"

"Don't let us keep you, it was nice meeting you, Ivy." Arden tipped his hat to her and strode off hand in hand with Kerry.

"They seem nice." Ivy was still surprised to be in a town where people knew their neighbors and actually wanted to stop and talk to each other.

"Kerry came to town shortly after me. You'll see her and her sister at the bridal shower." Sarah said as she waved to another couple walking on the opposite side of the street.

Ivy couldn't help staring at the man, his skin was pewter colored, unlike anything she had ever seen. This town became more and more interesting with every step she took.

They passed a butcher shop with a sign above the door that had a large werewolf tearing into a large piece of meat. She didn't stop because the smell of sugar enticed her to walk further. She glanced through the window and couldn't help the smile that spread across her face. Every square inch of the bakery was covered in different shades of pink and purple. The ceiling was painted to look like a sunny day with large, fluffy clouds.

Sarah looped her arm through Ivy's. "We'll have to eat here soon, you will love everything you try. My personal favorite is the cinnamon rolls."

Adam had walked ahead and came back to them. "They have a table ready for us."

Ivy's mouth was watering at the sight of all the baked goods. She groaned as she managed to pull herself away. She knew Alex was starving, and she didn't want to be responsible for his hangry side coming out.

Adam and Alex sat down at the first table in front of the restaurant.

Sarah picked Zeus up. "Before you sit, let's go to the bathroom, you've got to see this place." She held the dog out to Adam. "We'll be back in a minute."

He reluctantly held his hands up and took the creature. Ivy watched as he turned it to face him and stared into its eyes. "We should take you to Seraphine, I am not convinced you are a dog."

Sarah grabbed her hand and pulled her inside. Ivy's mouth hung open in amazement. She was instantly transported under the sea, complete with a pirate ship in one corner and aquariums spread throughout.

"This place is insane, you were not kidding when you said this town was eclectic." Ivy's eyes zipped back and forth, trying to take everything in.

Like a kid at Disney World, she took in every detail as they made their way through the restaurant and back to the bathroom. Ivy took the first stall and sat down. "I am starting to get why you moved here. After all the crap that happened in the city, I can see where this would be a fun to place to start fresh."

Sarah chuckled from the stall next to her, "I know right, plus this has been so good for Alex. He can be a little boy here."

Ivy paused as she caught sight of the toilet paper holder, "Um, Sarah, what the hell is that green stuff, and where do they expect me to put it?"

"Oh, geez, I forgot to warn you. The left side is regular toilet paper, the right side is kelp."

Ivy's upper lip curled in disgust. "Seriously? That's gross."

"I think it's nice they are trying to be inclusive of the aquatic people too."

She knew Sarah couldn't see her through the stall wall between them. That didn't stop her from turning and giving her a *are you nuts* look.

"I'm just kidding... it's there to add to the effect of the restaurant."

Ivy finished quickly and got out. She washed her hands in the giant seashell shaped sinks waiting for Sarah. coco

"You guys don't have a witch who lures kids into her candy house do you?"

Sarah walked up to the sinks. "No silly, it isn't a house, Alizon has a candy store down the street."

Ivy stared at her friend as if she had two heads. "Okay, you are starting to scare me."

Sarah shrugged at her cousin. "They love the paranormal around here, what's the harm in them going all out?" She opened the door to the bathroom and led her out.

They returned to the table to see Zeus sitting on the table, having a stare off with Adam.

Adam broke contact first and looked up at Ivy. "I looked up what a Cwn Annwn was, and I think you're safe. I don't think it is one of the Lord of the Underworld's hunting dogs. I tried some commands in Celtic, and he didn't seem to understand, so I'm confident he's not one of those."

Ivy was getting better at hiding the look of shock on her face when someone said something crazy. "Oh...that's a relief." She mumbled dryly.

She picked Zeus up and sat down, he instantly curled into a ball on her lap.

The door of the restaurant opened, a gorgeous woman who looked like she was glowing came out and walked towards them. Her long blonde hair hung to her waist, it looked like it was floating. Ivy resisted leaning closer to get a better view of the girl's legs beneath the gossamer skirt. It looked as if they were covered in scales, she respected her commitment to the theme. "Adam, Sarah, it's good to see you both, and hello Sir Alexander."

"Hi Nerissa, how's it been going?" Adam asked.

The ethereal woman stood gracefully next to Ivy. "Business has been good. I finally let Tristan into the kitchen, and I won't admit it to my brother, but he is an amazing cook."

Alex reached up and tugged gently on the woman's skirt. "Miss Nerissa, can I play with Cuddles?"

She looked to Sarah and waited for her to nod before brushing her hair off her shoulder and reaching up to grab something.

Ivy gasped as Nerissa brought a blue crab up to her face. "Be nice to Sir Alexander, or I will tape your claws shut." She paused for a second. "I know he's your friend and you wouldn't hurt him, but I know how excited you get sometimes."

She nodded at her pet and put it gently into Alex's waiting hands. "Now, what can I get you all."

Thank god she didn't look at Ivy first. *Everyone in this town is cuckoo for Cocoa Puffs*. She recovered quickly and glanced down at the menu. "I'll have a coke and the fried shrimp platter."

She handed over the menu, and people watched as the rest of the group ordered. "There's your friend, he must already be done in the apartment."

The group turned and watched the man walking down the sidewalk. Sarah smiled and looked back at Ivy. "Oh, I should have mentioned he's an identical twin."

"There are two of them?" She didn't mean to fan herself, but they were fine specimens of men and to have two of them equal in beauty and muscle was a fantasy come true.

Adam waved his hand toward the man and yelled, "Pascal."

The giant smiled and walked over. "Hey guys, and this must be the cousin who is in the apartment Toussaint is working on?"

"Hi, I'm Ivy." She waved.

He bowed slightly, "It's nice to meet you." He reached down and scratched the crab on its back. Apparently, it's normal to have a pet crab out and about town. "I have a feeling I'm not going to see much of my brother over the next week." He winked at Ivy.

Sarah laughed at Ivy's blush. "I heard my fiancé is really putting up a fight about having a bachelor party?"

"He can try all he wants to get out of it, but it's happening Wednesday whether he likes it or not. While you guys are having fun at your bridal shower, we'll be galivanting around town trying our best to get Adam to loosen up."

Adam quirked his eyebrow at his friend. "All I requested was that it be a nice, quiet dinner. I know you and Toussaint, and you don't know how to do anything nice or quiet."

Pascal rolled his eyes. "Don't worry. It's going to be exactly what you need."

Four

Toussaint stood back and inspected his work. The wall looked good as new, not like a witch had accidentally blown a giant hole in it.

The door of the apartment swung open, he turned and watched Ivy and her *dog* come in. He was surprised by the nerves running through his body. It had been a while since he had dated a woman and even then, they looked nothing like her. Usually, he went for the buxom redheads. Ivy had a short blonde bob that looked like she meant business and he was pretty sure a good, strong wind could blow her over. After a few seconds he realized he was staring, clearing his throat he said, "Hey there, it just needs a coat of paint and it will be all done. I tried to be out of your way before you got back, but time got away from me. If you have errands or something tomorrow, I can do it while you're gone?"

She waved him off, "Don't worry about being in the way. You can finish it today or tomorrow regardless of whether I'm here or not. Just give me a heads up, so I'm not walking around in jammies when you come in."

Toussaint didn't mean to, but he immediately started picturing her in her nightgowns, they were silky and small and probably not what she considered pj's. "I'll clean this mess up then I'll be gone. If you'd like I can bring some bagels or something over in the morning and finish up?"

He didn't know what made him offer up food to this complete stranger who probably wanted him to go away.

She set the dog down and started digging in her purse. "I was told the cinnamon rolls at Magical Delights Bakery are amazing. Is that on your way? I can give you some money to get a few?"

Toussaint glanced down, the dog had walked over and sat at his feet. He assumed its eyes were looking up at him. He couldn't tell through the tufts of hair everywhere. "Hey, buddy."

The dog yipped and ran behind Ivy's legs. He shrugged, "You are well informed, they are amazing, and I'll bring some with me. Is ten a.m., okay?"

She held out a twenty-dollar bill. "I can manage to make myself presentable by then."

He held his hand up, "It's my treat for not having the wall done before you got here." He knew at this point he was dragging the conversation out because he was enjoying talking to her. Then he remembered his vow to stay single. "I'll be out of your hair in a minute."

He turned back to his toolbox and started putting everything away. Out of the corner of his eye, he watched her grab her suitcase and head for the bedroom.

Zeus followed closely behind till she crossed the threshold of the hallway and continued on into the bedroom. Seconds later the creature howled like a banshee, it spun in circles and threw an outright tantrum.

Toussaint stared at the beast, trying to figure out what was happening.

"Oh relax, I needed to put my stuff down." Ivy reappeared and picked the dog up who immediately settled down.

She kissed and cuddled it for a few seconds before glancing up and seeing him staring at her. "Yeah...he doesn't like tile. The carpet stopped so he couldn't follow me any longer."

Toussaint stared at her dumbfounded. "So you have to carry him around any room with tile?"

"Yep, he has little quirks, I have mine, and we accept each other."

"He's an interesting character, isn't he? Did you get him from a breeder?" He closed his eyes for a second. Why didn't he just grab his stuff and go? Why did he continue to make idle conversation?

The dog looked up and licked her chin. "No, one day I was leaving for work, and this little guy was sitting at my front door. He had no tags, no microchip, and after a few weeks of flyers looking for an owner with no luck, I decided to keep him."

"Everything happens for a reason, you were obviously meant to keep him." he shrugged. "You never know, he could be your spirit animal or familiar. Do you have any witches in your ancestry?"

She looked at him dumbfounded. "Um, no, not that I know of."

"I guess you're just lucky then." He picked up the toolbox at his feet. "I'll see you in the morning."

As soon as he was out the door, he let out a growl. The first woman who had caught his attention in a long while, and she had to be human. Everything was more complicated with them. He loved Sarah, but he also remembered how poorly she took the news that they were real paranormal creatures. He wasn't sure the tiny wisp of a woman could survive in their world. He was a gargoyle, they weren't exactly known for their gentle touch.

He shook his head at himself, why was he even considering it. He vowed to stay single, and by god, one tiny woman wasn't going to change that.

Five

The knock on Ivy's door came right at ten a.m. on the dot. She appreciated that Toussaint was dependable and on time. She checked her hair and makeup one last time in the bathroom mirror before letting him.

She had been planning to wear yoga pants and a tank top today because she had to go shopping for some bridal shower supplies but thinking about the hunk that was coming over she had opted for a cute sundress with tiny daisies all over it.

She opened the door and smiled at both the man and the large box he was holding, which was teasing her with delicious smells. God, she loved pastries, almost as much as sex, but since she got way more baked goods than sex, they were pretty closely tied.

Toussaint held the box out to her. "Morning, I hope you're hungry."

If only he knew what she had been thinking about, he'd realize she hungered for food and him. She'd never had a casual fling before. She was only in town a week, he was hot, and based off the ringless finger she hoped single. Maybe he'd be open to helping a single girl out.

She grabbed the box and stepped back to let him in. He set a paint can down and turned to look at Zeus who had come up and sat at his feet. "I have a surprise for you, I'll be right back."

Ivy sat on the couch and dug into the warm, gooey, deliciousness as she waited curiously for him to return.

A minute later, he came back in with a giant roll of something slung over his shoulder. He pulled a box cutter out of his pocket and went towards the hallway where the bedroom was.

Ivy leaned forward to watch, she was thoroughly confused.

Toussaint unrolled the material and cut a couple of two-foot-wide strips. He laid one of them from the edge of the carpet to the bedroom and then took the rest into the room. Ivy hopped up and went to see what he was doing.

She knew she was being an idiot, but when she figured out what was happening tears sprang to her eyes. Toussaint had made a couple of carpet runners so Zeus could go in the bedroom on his own and go right up to the bed.

Zeus sniffed at the carpet line for a second before tentatively stepping on it and walking over to where Toussaint was taping the edge down by the bed.

Toussaint turned to the dog, "There you go, now you can go wherever your mommy goes." He looked up at Ivy. "I'll leave a couple of pieces in the hall closet in case there is another spot you need to cover for him."

Ivy stood there chewing on the food in her mouth. If she wasn't turned on by him before she sure as hell was now. She was used to people reacting badly toward her furry best friend but rarely did she see someone treat him with compassion.

She swallowed, then cleared her throat. "That is so sweet of you."

He shrugged, "It's not a big deal, we have a lot of extra materials laying around our warehouse, and I figured since you are going to be here for a few days, you might as well be comfortable."

For a few seconds neither spoke, just stood there looking at each other till she finally broke first. "Did you get a chance to eat? I hope all of those cinnamon rolls aren't for me?"

"You can have them all if you want." He shrugged. "I wouldn't mind having one or two of them though."

She spun on her heel and made her way back to the couch. Toussaint sat in the recliner across from her and grabbed a roll. It was quiet for a few minutes while they chewed.

Ivy desperately tried to think of something to say when an idea occurred to her. "Is there a lumber yard or home improvement store in the area-" she lost her train of thought for a second as he put his thumb and then finger in his mouth and sucked the cream cheese frosting off of them. "-I can get some wood from?"

He quirked an eyebrow at her, she realized it was an odd request. "At the bridal shower, we're going to be making these really cool wood signs everyone can customize and take home."

He looked surprised, "You're painting wood? Not drinking and hiring a stripper?"

Ivy rolled her eyes. "How very cliche of you. Sarah is not a partier. Her ex had an issue with alcohol, so she tends to stay away from it. Plus she loves to craft, so this will be perfect."

"Maybe we need to tone down Adam's bachelor party..." he looked off to the side for a second thinking. "I'll talk to the guys about it. So, what kind of wood do you need? As I said, I have a lot of supplies in our warehouse so I'm sure I can get whatever you need."

She tried to not read too much into his offer, maybe he was just being friendly and not trying to come up with ways to spend more time with her. "I don't know much about wood. I know it needs to be smooth, and I need to cut it into twelve inches by twelve-inch squares. I googled it, all I need to do is get a couple of sheets of plywood, buy a saw to cut them, then buy a sander to smooth them down and we'll be good to go."

She didn't appreciate the look of exasperation on his face.

"You are going to buy a bunch of tools and attempt something you googled?"

She shrugged, "I'm a strong, independent woman, I am confident I can figure it out." She nodded her head matter of factly at him.

He studied her for a second, "How about this, I'll paint the wall really quick then we'll go to the shop for supplies, and I'll help you. I have all the tools you'll need so no need to waste any money."

Ivy resisted dancing in her seat, no way was she going to turn down help from him. If she was lucky, he would get sweaty and need to take his shirt off. "If you have time, I would really appreciate the help."

He stood up. "I am part of the wedding party so really I have a duty to help make this perfect for them."

"While you paint, I'll check my work email, and we can go when you're ready."

Ivy went back to the bedroom, grabbed her cell phone and laptop. She couldn't help the broad smile that crossed her face when she stepped on the new carpet runner he created. She wanted a front seat view to watch him work, so she made her way back to the couch.

The first thing she did was text, Sarah.

Ivy: Hey Cuz, Toussaint's here painting then he agreed to help me with a few bridal shower errands. Is he single?

Sarah: Morning! I'm surprised you didn't ask me that question yesterday. He is single, but I'll warn you he is pretty happy as a bachelor. From what I can tell, he has no interest in getting serious.

Ivy: Challenge accepted. I'll see you tonight for dinner. Also, can you guys watch Zeus while I'm running my errands? He can stay alone in the apartment when we go for dinner.

Sarah: I'll send Adam down in a bit, he has a key, so if you are gone already he'll grab him and bring him upstairs. Have fun and do more than I would do!

She glanced up, her mouth went dry. Toussaint was painting the top edge of the wall by the roof. As he stretched his shirt lifted and she got a sneak peek of the smooth, tan skin of his lower back.

***

Over the next hour, Ivy answered emails and ogled her handyman. He was much better to watch than her superintendent in the city. That man had a giant beer belly, and when his shirt lifted up, she saw butt crack and hair.

Ivy's attention was pulled from the email she was typing when Toussaint hammered the paint can lid back on. "Done already?"

"I might need to do a second coat. This needs to dry then we'll see." He threw away the roller and packed up his gear. "Do you want to follow me in your car or I can give you a ride and drop you back here later?"

"I'm happy to ride you...er...ride with you." She wasn't sure who was more stunned by her slip of the tongue. That had to be the definition of a Freudian slip, and she was mortified.

He was obviously a gentleman, he ignored her gaffe and walked to the door.

So much for being subtle, if he didn't think she was interested before he had to now. Now to keep herself under control while she went and checked out his wood. If she was lucky, she'd get her hands on his power tool.

Ivy laughed at her innuendo's as she locked up the apartment and followed him to his truck. Lord help her, she was turning into a hornball, and she didn't have time for that, she had a bridal shower to get ready for.

Six

You are such an idiot. Toussaint was yelling at himself for the third time that morning. For someone who was trying to avoid relationships, he was sure putting himself within arm's length of the most tempting woman he had met in seventy-five years.

They pulled up to the architecture business he owned with his twin brother and steeled himself for the looks he was going to get. When Pascal found out he was willingly helping with shower errands, he was going to tease him mercilessly.

"Let's go around the back, there's a side entrance directly into the warehouse." Maybe if he was lucky, he could avoid being caught at all.

Toussaint grabbed the large metal rolling door and pushed it up. "All the wood is in the back corner, follow me."

Ivy whistled, "You were not kidding, I think you could give Home Depot a run for their money."

He looked through a few stacks of wood before pulling out a large sheet of plywood. "How many squares do we need?"

"Penny is bringing the stencils, and I didn't ask her how many she made. Let's make twenty just to be safe."

Toussaint squinted his eyes for a second, trying to do the math. "This sheet will have enough for thirty-two, so we'll be good to go and if Penny says we need more we can always come back."

He was aware how many times he said 'we' as if he was now firmly a part of their plan and he wasn't happy with himself. "Follow me."

They made their way over to the tool area, he handed her safety goggles and laid the wood down on the table. "Would you like to do the honors?" He held the circular saw out to her.

She stared at it for a second like it was a snake. "If you show me what to do I'll try it."

He held a finger up, telling her to wait a second. He jogged over to the wall and grabbed an apron. He stood in front of her and slipped it over her head, he liked that she only had to tilt her head a little to look into his eyes. "You don't want sawdust all over your dress."

She turned her back to him, "Can you tie the strings for me?"

Heat rushed Toussaint's...face. The back of her dress was a deep V, he wanted to brush his fingers across her pale white skin. He reached down for the strings and let his knuckles graze her hips and lower back as he tied it in a bow.

She turned back, her cheeks were pink, he hoped that meant she was affected the same way he was. "Okay, Teach, teach me."

***

Over the next three hours, they talked about every topic under the sun while they cut out the squares then sanded them one by one. He'd answered a few texts from his brother who was not happy he 'called in sick' when they were doing a big restoration job on the church.

He hated to admit it, but he had a lot of fun and didn't want the day to end. He had never dated a human before, and he was annoyed that he was considering breaking his vow now.

After all of the torture, his brother went through when he lost his mate, Toussaint swore he would never put himself in that situation. He and his brother had done fine for the last two hundred years, so why mess with what works?

Ivy stretched and cracked her back. "I can't believe we're done, how are you not sore all the time."

"I've been doing construction for a long time, I guess I've gotten used to it."

She hung the apron back on the wall. "I'm having dinner with Adam and Sarah if you'd like to join us. It will be my treat for all your help today."

"If you don't think they'd mind I'd be happy to join you." *Really you idiot, you made it thirty seconds before agreeing to spend more time with her.* Toussaint was apparently a glutton for punishment.

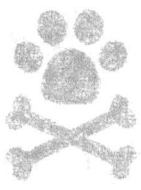

Seven

Ivy was sure she was going to have calluses on her hands, and there was no way she didn't have a splinter or two. Despite all of that, she had had a great time. She couldn't imagine how long that would have taken her had she done it alone.

They set the last of the wood squares on her dining room table. Ivy still wasn't sure how Toussaint had managed to carry fifteen to her five. Construction definitely did a body good.

"Penny had given me the number for Derrick who runs the Italian restaurant. I placed a catering order with him. I thought since that's where we're having dinner tonight we could go a little early and I can make sure everything is set." She arched her back, working the sore muscles. "I didn't get the name of the restaurant, is there more than one in town or do I need to text her?"

Toussaint laughed loudly. "What a bunch of chickens, no one would tell you the name?"

Ivy didn't understand how that was funny, she didn't think they had purposely withheld the name, but now he had her wondering. "Why would they hide it?"

"Let's just say some people struggle to eat there because of what it's called."

Ivy was perplexed, what could possibly be so bad to make people not eat there? "So, what's it called?"

Toussaint shook his head at her. "I think I'll save it as a surprise. It's over by the bakery, do you want to walk or drive?"

Ivy tried to think back to when she was at the bakery the day before. She had noticed there was another restaurant past Scales and Tails. She was so fascinated by the pace they were eating that she hadn't bothered to check it out. Between the kelp toilet paper, blue crab, and meeting Toussaint's twin, she had been pretty distracted. "I'm good with walking if you are, this town is fascinating, and this will give me a chance to see more of it."

"Do you want to tell Sarah we're meeting them there, then we'll go?"

Ivy grabbed her phone and texted Sarah.

Ivy: Thanks again for letting Toussaint crash our dinner, I wanted to pay him back for his help today. I want to check on the catering order for the shower, so we're going early. We'll wait at the bar till you get there.

Sarah: Sounds good, we'll drop Zeus off before we go. Have fun!

Ivy dropped her phone into her purse. "All set, lead the way."

Black Hollow was by far the smallest town Ivy had ever been in. After a captivating fifteen-minute walk, they arrived at the restaurant. "Are you kidding me?"

Toussaint gave her a goofy smile but said nothing.

She made a silent, gagging motion. "That is disgusting, now I have the mental image in my mind, and it's killing my appetite."

"The Rotten Meatball is the best Italian food I've ever had in my life. I promise if you can forget about the name, it will be the most delicious meal of your life."

She shuddered, "Okay, I'm trusting you."

What kind of person would name their restaurant after a rotting anything? You're supposed to entice your customers to come in. She understood the town was quirky, but surely, she wasn't the only one who was grossed out? Black Hollow was getting stranger and stranger by the minute. What was she going to see next?

Eight

Toussaint held the door open for Ivy, the smell of garlic instantly had his mouth watering. Italian was never a good idea for a first date. Not that this was a date, but no one wants to have funky breath for that first kiss.

He let out a small sigh of frustration at himself. He had to stop thinking about her in any other way than a temporary guest in town.

Ivy turned and smiled up at him. "I haven't eaten anything yet and I've already forgiven them for the name. I can smell how good this is going to taste and oh my god, are we in Italy? I feel like we just entered a Tuscan village."

Toussaint smiled at her enthusiasm, he'd been in Black Hollow so long he forgot about the excitement people got when they first arrived. Most of the residents never leave again once they settle here. That doesn't mean they don't miss the bigger world around them. The business owners had banded together years ago and agreed to make their shops as unique, authentic, and fun as possible. He took pride in knowing he and his brother had helped rebuild almost every business on the main street.

Toussaint rested his hand on the small of her back, "Derrick is sitting over there in the corner, he would love to hear how much you like the restaurant."

As they made their way over to Derrick, multiple people called out to Toussaint saying hi. When paranormals first moved to town they were usually quiet and withdrawn. Rarely did they trust anyone and it took years for them to come out of their shells. Too many years of having to hide their true selves caused them to be very reserved.

He wanted to stop and introduce Ivy to each table, but she was a woman on a mission and was marching toward Derrick. She really took her Maid of Honor duties seriously.

The brunette eating at the table glanced up and smiled at them. Toussaint had only met her a handful of times. She seemed nice enough. "Derrick, Raveena, this is Ivy. She is hosting the bridal shower for Sarah."

Derrick glanced up from the computer he had been working on. "Sarah, it's nice to meet you in person." He stood and held his hand out to shake hers.

Toussaint realized he should have warned Ivy ahead of time. He heard her gasp then cover it quickly by clearing her throat. "Hi, it's nice to finally meet you too."

Obviously, the zombie had gotten used to people staring at his shiny, silver skin. He didn't say a word as he let Ivy study him for a few seconds.

Toussaint broke the silence first, "You wanted to review the catering order, right?"

Ivy blinked a few times, her eyes focused on the group again. "Yes, sorry, I am excited for tomorrow. Penny said you're going to deliver everything to Seraphine's house?"

Toussaint's head snapped toward Ivy, he had no idea that's where the party was going to be. Seraphine was the town matriarch, she founded Black Hollow and protected everyone who lived there. No one really knew what paranormal creature she was, she seemed to be all seeing and all knowing, at least that was Toussaint's way of explaining her. He was shocked that she would let a stranger into her home.

In the past, when a human came to town, it was usually because they were meant to be there and Seraphine helped orchestrate getting them there. He doubted she had anything to do with Sarah choosing her as her Maid of Honor, but crazier things have happened.

As the group continued their conversation, Toussaint tuned them out. He tried to squelch the giddiness that surged through him at the idea Ivy may not be a temporary visitor. Maybe she was here for him after all. The memory of his brother after he lost his mate came surging to Toussaint's mind. It was enough to help him steal his heart against any more thoughts of him having a future with Ivy. Love wasn't worth the risk.

Nine

Ivy stared at the ceiling of her temporary bedroom. Her eyes burned from lack of sleep. Her mind had been racing all night trying to make sure she was prepared for the party.

After a great dinner with Toussaint, Sarah, and Adam, they walked home, and Toussaint abruptly left without even walking her to her door. Instead of wallowing in thoughts as to why he did that she decided to focus on the bridal shower. Once she was confident she had prepared everything possible, she crawled under the fluffy comforter and tried to sleep. The moon was high by the time she managed to shut her brain down. It wasn't until an unfortunate trip to the bathroom just after dawn allowed her mind to wake up again just enough to torture her with more thoughts about her to-do list.

She groaned when her alarm went off, her hand groped around the side table till she found the phone and shut the offensive noise off. She laid there another ten minutes before her phone started buzzing.

She gave in and sat up, with one eye barely open she stared at the bright screen and tried to read the text. Her vision finally focused, it was a message from Penny saying they were checked into the Inn and she would be there in thirty.

Accepting she wasn't going to get any more sleep, she showered and dressed quickly. She prided herself on her no-fuss prep routine and ability to be ready in fifteen minutes flat.

By the time Zeus was fed and walked, Penny was pulling into the parking lot. She hopped out of her car with way more pep than Ivy was feeling. "Are you ready to get this party started?"

"How many coffees have you had and why didn't you bring me any?" Ivy pouted.

Penny shrugged. "I've only had two and what kind of friend would I be if I didn't bring you some. There is a cup in my car ready for you when we get on the road." She bent down and picked Zeus up. "How's my favorite beasty doing?"

The dog licked her face eagerly, he had a serious addiction to coffee, and since it wasn't good for him Ivy didn't let him have any. That didn't stop him from trying to lick any remnants possible from around Penny's mouth.

"Help me load the car then we can get going. You're sure Seraphine doesn't mind us coming this early to set up?"

Penny set the dog down and started walking towards the apartment. "I promise you she is fine with it. She practically demanded we have the party at her place and no one says no to her."

They got to the door at the same time as Adam and Alex. "We're here to help you guys load the car then if you are okay with it, Zeus is going to hang with us today."

Ivy couldn't help smiling at his tone. "None of that is actually your idea, right?"

"You gave up your week to be here, giving my future wife a bridal shower and helping her with the wedding. Anything I can do to help you make her happy, I will do gladly."

Ivy's heart melted, he had slowly been growing on her, but that pushed her over the line. She was team Adam all the way now and was finally feeling good with the idea of them getting married after such a short time together.

"Oh, he's good." Penny sighed.

Ivy nodded in agreement before opening the door. "Toussaint was able to carry fifteen of these wood signs, think you can beat that?"

"Pfft...just because I run the newspaper doesn't mean I'm a couch potato." He held out his arms. "Start stacking, and if I do beat him, I hope you'll rub it in his face."

Ivy and Penny looked at each other and rolled their eyes. Ivy secretly rooted for Adam to win, it would give her the perfect excuse to see Toussaint again. "Okay big guy, let's see how strong you are."

Ten

Toussaint sat in his car, staring at his phone in dismay. Adam texted their group chat and said the bachelor party was off and he needed everyone at the apartment immediately.

He turned and looked at his passengers, "Well, ladies, I guess I won't be needing you after all." The plastic blow-up dolls stared back at him, their mouths in a wide O shape. "I know, I'm shocked too."

He tossed his phone on the passenger seat and chuckled as it slid between the legs of the blonde doll sitting there. "Don't get all excited the next time the phone vibrates."

He looked at himself in the rearview mirror and shook his head. "You clearly need to get laid."

He drove straight to the apartment and took the stairs up to the door two at a time. Adam was not a dramatic guy, so Toussaint knew something was wrong.

He knocked twice then stormed inside and stopped. "Oh my god, what happened? Did one of the unicorns explode in here?"

Adam sat on the couch, his head in his hands. Sebastian, the town Sheriff, was sitting next to him, patting him on the back.

The groom-to-be groaned. "It's so much worse than that."

Toussaint tried to figure out what was worse than exploding unicorns but came up empty.

Sebastian saved him from guessing. "Apparently Adam isn't a very good dog sitter, and Zeus has an affinity for flowers and candles."

Toussaint walked around the room, trying to figure out what everything was. Tulle, tissue paper, flowers, and chunks of something white were everywhere.

Alex walked back into the apartment, carrying Zeus. "He didn't get sick."

Adam looked up, a little less panicked looking. "Well, at least I didn't let her best friend's pet die." He grabbed a big chunk of white off the coffee table and held it up. "Sarah has been working for weeks on these favors and decorations. It only took the dog forty-five minutes to destroy it all. She's going to be devastated."

Toussaint felt terrible for the guy, he had waited hundreds of years for the right woman to come along. He had never seen the other man so happy, he had come out of his shell since being with her. Toussaint didn't agree with marriage. That didn't mean he didn't want the best for Adam. "We've got hours before the girls are done with their shower. I'll text the guys, and we'll have this good as new before they get home."

Sebastian, Alex, and Adam all stared at him in shock. If he can build a structure from the ground up, he sure as hell could make a few centerpieces. "Start cleaning up and I'll rally the troops."

He walked over to Adam's desk and grabbed a pen and paper. He studied the room one more time then started making notes of what supplies they needed and who he was assigning each item too. Once he had the list ready to go, he went down the line and called each person.

There was no place like Black Hollow. Everyone in it had been alienated for so long till they found their home there. Now they jumped at the opportunity to help each other out.

By the time they had the apartment clean and work area's assembled, people started showing up. Toussaint smiled at the assembled group. What do you get when you combine a mummy, a zombie, a phoenix, a sorcerer, a yeti, a zombie, a cupid, one human and a bunch of gargoyles? The best damn wedding crew in town, at least in his humble opinion.

"Everyone pick a station, we've only got a couple of hours and a steep learning curve. According to *Google*, there is a website called *Pinterest* that we can use to get ideas."

Saroj held his hand up to get everyone's attention. "I use *YouTube* too, you can watch videos of people making almost anything."

Toussaint nodded and smiled at the gentle giant. While the rest of the group looked nauseous at the idea of what they were being asked to do the Yeti was excited. "That's the spirit, now let's channel Martha Stewart and rock this fluff."

Eleven

Ivy's jaw dropped lower and lower as Penny got closer to Seraphine's "house". The wrought iron gates stood ten feet tall. As they pulled up, the massive stone gargoyles standing sentry on either side slowly rotated their heads, so they were looking into the car. Penny rolled her window down.

The mouth of the statue on the driver side opened, a mechanical voice spoke loudly, causing Ivy to jump. "Who disturbs my slumber?"

Penny chuckled, "Really, stealing lines from *Aladdin* now?"

The statue didn't move, the mouth hung open waiting.

Penny sighed, "Penny and Ivy are here to set up for the bridal shower per *Seraphine's* instructions."

Apparently, name dropping was the trick, the statue rotated back to its original position, and the gate opened silently.

Penny rolled the window of her car up. "That has to be the fastest I've ever gotten through the gate."

"Her staff really take their guard duty seriously don't they?"

Penny gave her a side eye. "You have no idea."

"This has to be the strangest town I've ever seen, and what was up with Derrick from the restaurant, his skin was silver and shined? You don't know what it took for me not to ask."

Penny shook her head at her. "That would have been a terrible first impression. Excuse me, sir, why do you glow like a Twilight vampire?"

Ivy stuck her tongue out at her friend. "I wouldn't have said it like that, but that is exactly what I wanted to ask. So, do you know?"

Penny shrugged, "I assumed it was some medical condition. I never asked."

Ivy couldn't fathom how she could just let it go like that. Maybe it was because as soon as you started questioning one thing about the town, you saw something else out of the ordinary and got distracted.

She craned her neck to look out the top of the windshield. The long, winding drive got eerier the deeper they went. The trees had no leaves, the bare branches were tangled overhead blocking the sunlight from coming through.

"Shut the front door." Ivy was stunned as she got her first look at Seraphine's place. "Seriously, who would call this a house? I'm pretty sure they filmed any number of horror films here." The stone mansion was dark and menacing looking except for the giant sconces lit with fire on both sides of the front doors.

Penny pulled right up to the doors and got out. As Ivy climbed out, she saw a tiny woman walking towards them. "Penny, it's so good to see you again. And this must be the lovely Ivy I've heard so much about."

The older woman stepped close and held her hands out to Ivy. Not sure what else to do she let her grab them. "You are lovely, aren't you? I knew something was pushing me to meet you, and now I see why." Seraphine smiled warmly, she had one purple eye and one green eye, Ivy had never seen anything like it. "You will be perfect, I knew this was going to be a good day."

Without any explanation, Seraphine spun on her heel and started walking back inside.

Ivy turned to Penny, completely lost as to what the woman had been rambling about. "Are you sure she should be living alone? Is she all there mentally?"

Penny got a horrified look on her face. "Oh my god, don't say that out loud." She shook her head at Ivy then turned and started pulling bags out of the car. "Now let's go cover this gothic mansion in lots of frilly lace and naughty toys."

**

Ivy finished hanging up the 'Pin the penis on the hunk' game just as the doorbell rang.

Penny stood back, hands on her hips, looking around. "I think we did awesome, now let's go meet our guests."

As they made their way to the door, Seraphine was already standing there waiting for them. It was the first time Ivy had seen the older woman since she waved them into the large dining room and told them they could set up.

Ivy lined up next to them and pasted on her best smile, these were Sarah's new friends, so Ivy wanted to make a good impression.

The door opened to a large group of women holding presents of varying sizes. Ivy wondered if they all drove together in a bus or were all just really good at being on time.

Seraphine nodded at each woman as they came inside. Penny said hello to each then introduced them to Ivy. "These two trouble makers are Alizon and Raveena, they are the ones that put that hole in your apartment.

Alizon owns the candy store on Main Street, and Raveena is the Head Librarian."

Raveena waved her off, "It was a tiny hole, and I actually got to meet Ivy last night at the restaurant. It's good to see you again."

"This adorable lady is Meddie, she owns the hair salon in town and will be doing our hair the day of the wedding."

Meddie reached up and ran her hands through Ivy's short blonde bob. "It's hard to improve upon perfection, but I'll do my best for all of you."

Ivy blushed at the younger woman's compliment. "I know I don't have much hair for you to work with, sorry."

Penny shoved her excitedly. "Oooh, you should put in really long extensions, that would be cool."

Before Ivy could respond, the girl was gone, and the next in line was ready to be introduced.

"Saoirse is the private assistant to Cade Osiris."

Ivy gasped, "No one told me he lives here. His clothes are amazing, you must love working for him."

Saoirse shrugged. "He's actually quite the pain in the ass. Half the time, he forgets to eat, and I have to remind him to sleep."

Ivy was impressed, "I wish I was so good at something that it consumed me like that. That is the passion you hear about, but I've not experienced myself."

The woman next to her spoke up. "It's gotten better since he got together with Silver, right?"

Saoirse nodded in agreement. "That's true, it turns out he loves sex just as much as designing clothes, so he has found a better balance."

The other woman laughed. "Amen to that, now I need to find a hunk for me to get it on with."

Penny huffed, "Vic, you are gorgeous, how can you possibly be single?" She turned towards Ivy, "Victoria works with her family, they own the Drakki jewelry business."

"Best diamonds in the world. If you like shiny baubles let me know, I'll hook you up."

"Are there women who don't like shiny baubles?" Ivy asked.

Vic shrugged. "Surprising, I know."

Another woman walked up to the door and came inside. "Diamonds are okay, but I prefer pearls. Something about those shiny, white stones gets me every time."

Vic quirked her eyebrow at her. "Maybe because you are a dentist and they remind you of teeth?"

The woman considered the idea for a second. "I never thought of it that way. You're probably right."

Penny chuckled. "This is Josephine, as you just heard she is the town's dentist."

Ivy suddenly felt nervous to smile. Do dentists go around judging people's smiles?

Seraphine glanced outside. "I think this is everyone, let's get settled while we wait for the guest of honor."

Twelve

Toussaint tossed down the glue gun he was holding. "I swear to god if I burn myself one more time I am throwing that dog out the window."

Pascal nodded in agreement as he sat there with his finger in a cup of ice water from the multiple burns he had given himself.

Derrick sighed loudly for the fifth time since he arrived. "I'll be lucky if I even have my hands when this is over. I'm sure when Alizon gave Raveena a spare key to her candy shop it wasn't with the intention I would go in and steal every ounce of chocolate she had in storage."

Liam cleared his throat. "Someone could have warned me to bring some charcoal briquettes with me. My throat is killing me, I've been blowing fire for two hours now trying to get all this chocolate melted to just the right temperature."

Seren and Saroj looked at each other and shrugged. The yeti patted Liam on the back, trying to help him cough. "I feel for you. I'm having a great time personally."

Cade set the bouquet down that he had finished, "I'm with you. My bows are on point, I could do this all day."

Sebastian rolled his eyes at the mummy. "How is it possible I can shoot a moving target with perfect accuracy, but I can't get these stupid roses into the shape of a heart?"

Aristide's shoulders slumped as he set down his decoration. His heart-shaped flowers looked more like an ice cream cone.

Silver sneezed. "While I don't appreciate being in charge of the flowers when you know I have allergies I still think it's better than Wendell over there."

The group turned and looked into the kitchen. It was a disaster zone; multiple cakes were discarded around the room in various states of destruction. There was one cake that sort of resembled something the girls would like, but the frosting was melting off, causing it to look like a dying clown.

Cupid raised a resentful gaze at the group staring at him. "If one of you fuckers say a word I will shoot you with my arrow and make sure you fall for the vilest human I can find."

The front door opened, Adam and Alex walked in laughing about something and drinking milkshakes. If looks could kill, they would be dead ten times over.

Aristide crossed his arms across his chest. "Someone explain to me why he keeps getting to leave while the rest of us sit here suffering? I mean, we were supposed to be drinking and causing havoc. Instead, I'm covered in glitter." He shuddered.

Adam held his hands up defensively. "I can't help it that I keep needing to buy cake supplies. By the way, Derrick, the grocery store is out of eggs, so I took some from The Rotten Meatball."

A loud crash in the kitchen had everyone turning to look. Wendell dropped a cake pan in the sink and stared them all down.

Adam leaned towards Toussaint and whispered, "Do I want to know?"

Toussaint shook his head but said nothing, he was way too scared of getting an arrow to the ass to say a word.

Alex skipped over to the couch, where Zeus had been happily napping for the last two hours. He gave the dog a rawhide bone and went back to his milkshake.

Sebastian huffed. "Even the fucking dog is getting a treat, and this is all his fault. When we're done here, drinks are on me at the bar."

Toussaint and Pascal high fived. The coolest part of a best friend who owns a bar is all the free drinks you can persuade him to give you.

Saroj held his hand up. "Question, why didn't we just have the unicorns at the bakery make one?"

Another loud crash from the kitchen had everyone laughing. Apparently, Wendell did not appreciate the question.

Toussaint stuck his burnt finger into the cup his brother was still holding. "The point of this was to replace it all without Sarah noticing anything."

The group looked around at their work. Pascal broke the silence first. "Well, we're fucked."

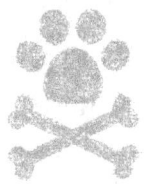

Thirteen

Ivy couldn't hold back the tears from welling in her eyes when she saw Sarah, her face shining with radiance and contentment. A couple of years ago, her cousin was living in a battered women's shelter and hiding from her husband. Now she was living in this surreal town where everyone seemed to be supportive of each other, and her soon to be husband seemed like he would treat her exactly how she was always meant to be treated.

As the group was finishing eating the fantastic food from The Rotten Meatball Penny stood up and waited for everyone's attention. "One of Sarah's favorite past times is crafting. I was thinking since she is new in town she could make a decoration for the home she is building with Adam."

Ivy opened a box on the floor behind Penny and pulled out a mound of aprons. "It wouldn't be fun if we watched her paint, so we're all going to make a sign."

Penny grabbed part of the pile and started walking around passing them out. "If you remember I sent you all a list of sayings you could put on your signs. I've printed the templates for you, and they are at your stations in the next room."

The group got up and followed the hostesses down the hall to a large ballroom. Tables had been set up around the room. The wood squares Toussaint and Ivy had worked on the day before were already laid out.

Ivy tied her apron behind her as she finished explaining the project. "On the table in the corner are bottles of paint. There are tiny paper cups you can use to take a small amount of paint back to your tables. You will paint the wood one solid color then take it over to the table in that corner," she turned on her heel and pointed across the room. "Use the hair dryers to dry the paint. It's critical you use the cold air setting, not the heat."

Penny held up one of the templates with a saying on it. "Once it's dry, bring it back to your table and carefully stick the stencil on. You will then paint the words and pictures however you'd like, then pull the stencil back off before it dries. Once you have all the template pieces off, you can take it back over to the dryers and finish the process."

"Penny and I have done these types of projects quite a few times so if you need help just wave us over and we'll help you. Sometimes the stencils can be a little tough to get on smoothly."

Sarah held up her template to inspect it. "I can't wait, this is such a great idea."

The rest of the group murmured their agreements then jumped right in.

After the hair dryers had been going for a while, Ivy noticed Vic was staring daggers at her stencil. Ivy took pity on her and went to help. "Having trouble?"

Vic sighed, "No matter how slowly I lay it down and smooth it, I keep getting air bubbles."

Ivy picked up the rubber scraping tool. "May I?"

Vic gladly stepped aside. "Please do."

As Ivy started at the top and slowly made her way down, she noticed for the first time what the template said. "Dragon's do it best?"

Vic shrugged, "They are my favorite paranormal creatures, so I thought I'd do something different."

Ivy always admired other people's creativity. Once she had the stencil smooth, she stepped aside and waved Vic back to her spot. "You're all set. When you are pulling the stencil off from around the dragon image, you may want to use the pick tool to get the tiny pieces up."

"Will do, thanks!"

Interested to see if the rest of the quirky town had chosen unique sayings, she walked around to see how everyone was doing.

Nerissa's table was next to Vic, Ivy peaked at the sign to see it read *Shifter's do it Best* with a large claw image next to it. The next couple of tables were pretty common sayings like *Live Laugh Love* and *Home is where the Heart is*. The last table was Raveena, she was just starting to paint over the stencil. Her sign read *Home is where the Casket is* with a picture of a casket on it.

Raveena noticed her watching, "I always joke with Derrick that he looks like a zombie when he comes home from the restaurant, so I thought this would be funny."

Ivy laughed and hoped it didn't sound fake. "Yeah, I'm sure he can be dead tired after work." She moved on and went back to her own station. She tried to never judge other people, but this whole town was so strange. People were quirky, and she loved that. Here there were so many peculiar people it flabbergasted her. How did so many of them manage to settle in the same small town?

Fourteen

Toussaint felt nauseous as they sat there, waiting for the girls to get home. He could only imagine how Adam was feeling at that moment. The rest of the impromptu wedding decorators went ahead to Stoney's while he and Adam stayed back to face the music.

The girl's laughter could be heard from the other side of the door just before it opened, and they walked in. Sarah paused in the doorway. "Why do you guys look really guilty?"

Adam unconsciously rubbed the back of his neck. "Let me start by saying how much I love you."

Toussaint rolled his eyes, that was not the best way to start.

Sarah and Ivy's expressions both instantly turned to alarm.

Adam realized his gaffe too late. "Don't worry, Alex and Zeus are fine."

"Zeus shouldn't be," Toussaint muttered.

He shrugged at Ivy's glare.

Sarah scanned the room, her eyes finally landing on the dining room table where all the decorations were laid out. Her head tilted, Toussaint knew it would be seconds before she figured out something was different.

She walked over and stared at the flowers, bows, and stacks of small boxes that had the chocolates in them. "I'm pretty sure none of this existed when I left this morning. Where is everything that was here?"

Adam sighed, his shoulders slumped. "You know I've been trying to teach Alex about computers. We were working in my office and totally forgot about Zeus who had been sleeping under the coffee table."

Ivy's hand covered her mouth, 'Oh no."

Adam glanced at her then back at Sarah. "It really was impressive how quickly he was able to destroy everything. I still haven't figured out how he got the cake off the kitchen counter."

Sarah gasped and ran over to the cake cover and lifted it. For thirty seconds, she stared down at the cake but didn't say a word. Toussaint's thumbnail was chewed almost entirely away as he sat there waiting for her to either explode or meltdown.

Ivy walked over to him. "Why are you covered in band-aids?"

He held his hand up and studied his bandaged fingers. "It turns out it takes a special person to be able to use hot glue guns, and honestly, I would gladly participate in rounding up everyone in existence and lighting them on fire."

Ivy's eyes rounded in shock. "I don't think I've ever heard vehemence for such a simple tool."

Sarah walked back to the kitchen table and sat down, still staring at everything. Toussaint didn't want to speak up and risk upsetting her further, he took the cowardly way and stayed back.

Ivy walked up and started moving things around, inspecting them. "These aren't terrible, but the good news is we have a few days. Between me, you, and Penny, we can redo anything you want."

Toussaint wanted to be offended, but he was a big enough man to admit they were no Martha Stewart.

Sarah finally turned and looked at Adam. "I'm trying really hard to figure out how you got all of this remade so fast?"

Adam glanced over to Toussaint before looking back at her. "Well, it was the strangest bachelor party ever. Toussaint rounded up the guys, and everyone came over and worked on something. We had no way to get that many candles, so we raided Alizon's place for supplies. Then Seren, Liam, Saroj, and Derrick made the chocolates and packaged them up." He held up one of the bouquets of flowers. "Silver and Cade worked on these. Sebastian and Aristide worked on the aisle decorations, Toussaint and Pascal made the centerpieces."

Sarah studied the objects again, "What about the cake?"

Adam grimaced and looked over to Toussaint. He decided to take pity on his friend and take the bullet on this one. "I thought Wendell would have the skillset to make a pretty cake...fourteen cakes later the town is out of eggs, and you have a somewhat recognizable replacement."

Tears poured down Sarah's face, he felt like shit for not doing better. Ivy surprised him by rubbing Sarah's back and defending them. "I think they did a brilliant job, it's not that bad, we can fix this."

Sarah shook her head, then wiped the tears from her face. "I don't care that they aren't perfect. They are as unique as the men who made them, and I honestly can't believe any of those guys sat here and did this for me. I wish you had pictures, it would have been a sight to see."

A collective sigh of relief went around the room. He should have realized Sarah wasn't a bridezilla and would never have thrown a fit.

The door to Alex's bedroom swung open, and Zeus came running out. Ivy scooped him up and held him up so she could look in his eyes. "You know better than this, why did you destroy Sarah's things?"

Toussaint couldn't understand why she sat there staring as if the dog was going to answer.

She turned back to Sarah, "I'm going to take him out, I'll be back in a few minutes."

Toussaint thought about asking if she wanted company then he remembered he was trying not to get too close to her.

He watched as she left the apartment with Alex skipping along behind her.

Thirty seconds later, a knock on the door had everyone turning in that direction. Toussaint opened it thinking Ivy was returning already. Instead he found Seraphine standing on the other side smiling serenely.

He turned and gave them a panicked look. He tried to think back, he wasn't aware of her ever going to anyone's house.

Sarah walked up, "Seraphine, come inside. Is everything okay? Did we leave something at your house?"

"Everything is fine, I actually have another present for you and wanted to give it to you together."

The mysterious woman walked in, glanced at the decorations then sat down on the couch. She pulled two small bottles out of her pocket and set them down in the center of the coffee table. The rest of the group huddled around, intrigued by the intricate vials in front of them.

"As you know Adam, you are immortal and Sarah, you are not. My wedding present to you is a choice. Adam can take the vile on the left and become a mortal, you can grow old together. Or Sarah can take the vile on the right and become immortal, you can be together for eternity."

She patiently waited for the group to process the bombshell she had just dropped on them.

Sarah gasped, "Oh my god, I never even thought about that. How are we getting married in a couple of days and hadn't talked about this?"

Adam didn't answer Sarah; instead, he stared at Seraphine. Toussaint was surprised by the anger in his voice. "You've been able to make me mortal all these years, and you let me suffer? You knew how miserable I was, and you let me continue this life of isolation and loneliness?"

Seraphine's smile didn't crack. "It wasn't time. Think about it, if I had given you the potion a hundred years ago you would be long dead and wouldn't have met Sarah and Alex."

Sarah's head whipped around to Seraphine. "Alex, what about my son? If I become immortal are you going to give him the potion too?"

Seraphine's smile finally dropped. "It's not Alex's time. Have faith that his path is set and you won't be disappointed."

Toussaint suddenly felt like an outsider to a very private conversation, he slipped out of the apartment without anyone noticing.

Ivy and Alex were coming up the stairs, he held his hands up to stop them. "They are having a private conversation; can we wait in your apartment till they are done?"

He saw the concern on Ivy's face, but she knew better than to get Alex worked up. "Sure, I think we have some leftover cake from the shower."

Alex jumped up and down excitedly, kids were easily distracted.

The trio and the furball made their way over to Ivy's apartment, she cut them each a slice of cake, and they sat at the kitchen table eating in silence.

He wanted to explain to her what was happening. She didn't know the truth of the town though so she wouldn't understand. And he was not going to be the one to tell her the truth. He heard how bad Sarah had taken it when she first found out, he had no interest in dealing with that drama.

As Alex chattered on and on replaying his day with Zeus, the grown-ups waited impatiently. Finally, a knock on the door had Ivy and Toussaint rushing over.

Sarah stood on the other side, her face red and swollen from crying. "Pack your things, we need to leave now."

Toussaint wanted to argue and ask questions, but women were different. Ivy didn't ask questions, she just did what her friend needed her to do.

Sarah walked in and ran over to Alex, he didn't say a word as she held onto him and cried. From what he knew of their time in the battered women's shelter, he wasn't surprised to see the boy rubbing her back and giving her comfort. He no longer looked like a little boy, he had obviously been through too much in his short lifetime.

Ivy ran around grabbing things and shoving them in bags, she waved to Toussaint to come into the bedroom.

She peeked out to make sure Sarah wasn't listening. "I don't know what happened but let me get her away from here and settled down. I'm sure we'll be back soon. Right now she needs to feel safe, and for her, that means escaping." She bent over the dresser and scribbled something then handed him a small square piece of paper. "Here's my cell number, text me your info. I'll let you know what's going on and you need to go check on Adam. I would expect he isn't doing very well right now either."

She grabbed her suitcase and made her way back to the living room. "I'm ready, let's go."

Sarah grabbed Alex's hand and pulled him along. She paused and looked up at Toussaint, "I'm sorry I have to think about Alex first."

With that, they left the apartment and drove away. Toussaint was in shock, in a matter of minutes they were gone. He stared around the apartment at the bridal shower decorations still laying around. He left and took the stairs two at a time, fear ran through him at what condition he would find Adam in.

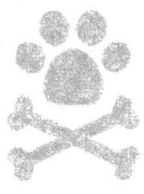

Fifteen

Ivy was calm as she drove away from Black Hollow. Over the years Sarah had called her for help escaping when Hank had beaten her up. She had gotten good at being able to jump into action and get them away.

She knew this was different, every bone in her body told her Adam was a good guy, and this was some kind of misunderstanding. She just needed to give Sarah time to process her own feelings, and when she was ready, she would open up and talk to her.

An hour from town, Ivy spotted a motel. "Let's stop here for the night, I know they are pet-friendly, and I will need to go back to the apartment to get the rest of my stuff." She hoped Sarah would buy that excuse, there was no need to go further away when she hoped things would get worked out quickly and they could get back in time for the wedding.

Sarah didn't say a word, just stared out the window. Ivy knew it would be a while before she told her anything. She ran into the lobby and got a room for the night with the option to add nights if needed.

Alex smiled sadly at her as she climbed back in the car, her heart broke for the little boy. "You get first dibs on which bed you want then you can decide what we do next."

They drove around the building and parked in front of their room. Zeus yipped as he jumped out of the car behind Alex and followed him to the door. As soon as Ivy had it open, Alex ran inside and jumped on the bed furthest from the door. Zeus put his front paws on the bed and waited to be picked up. Ivy tossed him up with the boy then went back out for her bag and the small one Sarah had brought with her.

Sarah got out of the car and walked mechanically to the room and laid down on the first bed.

This was bad. What the hell happened in the ten minutes she was downstairs?

Right after they turned on the highway, Toussaint had texted her saying to be careful. She sat on the edge of the bed and pulled out her phone.

Ivy: We stopped at the motel off the highway. Did Adam fill you in? Do you know what happened?

Toussaint: He has said a lot, but I have no idea what he is saying. Apparently, he speaks German and big surprise, I don't. If he doesn't calm down soon, I'm going to try alcohol and see if I can mellow him out enough to get him to switch back to English.

"German?" Ivy muttered.

Ivy: Sarah hasn't said a word since we left, it will probably be tomorrow before she talks.

Good luck with Adam and let me know if you get details that may help me.

Toussaint: Will do, good luck to you too.

Ivy turned and laughed as she listened to Alex's innocent giggle as Zeus stood on his chest and licked his face. Whatever happened had to do with Alex, and she was dying to know the truth, but she was going to have to be patient.

"Alex, let's go grab some dinner, and we'll bring some back for your mom." She walked over to Sarah. Her cousin was staring out the window. Ivy doubted she saw anything. She brushed the hair from her face. "We'll be back soon, rest for now. Zeus is going to stay here and cuddle with you."

Without her having to say anything, the dog jumped across the beds and curled up behind Sarah's knees. "Watch over her, I'll bring you back a treat." The dog closed its eyes and went to sleep. She wished Sarah could find that peace even if only for a couple of hours. They usually had all the time in the world to get her through these episodes, but there was supposed to be a wedding in less than forty-eight hours, so she had very little time to get her through this and back to Adam.

Sixteen

Toussaint's head was throbbing, he wanted to die, and for some reason, he was cuddling a stuffed dinosaur.

After two hours of listening to Adam rant in German, he got Pascal to come help get him to Stoney's bar. They didn't know what else to do, so they got him plastered. After his fifth whiskey, the German had subsided, but he still wasn't explaining what happened. Between sips, he muttered about how much he loved Sarah, and he would do whatever she wanted as long as he was with her.

It was two in the morning before Sebastian was able to close up and help him get Adam back to the apartment. Unfortunately, Toussaint had matched him drink for a drink, so he passed out in Alex's bed.

As slowly as possible, he got up and made his way to the living room. He found Adam sitting on the couch with Wendell's cake in his lap, and it was half eaten.

Cupid was going to kill them both.

Toussaint approached slowly as if he were a wounded animal. "Hey, buddy, why don't we put the cake down before you bring it all back up."

Adam cuddled the plate closer to his chest. "What does it matter, she isn't coming back. I waited three hundred years for love, and I lost it. I might as well take the potion to make me mortal, so I can at least put myself out of my misery." He reluctantly let go of the cake as Toussaint pulled it from his grasp. "And I haven't forgiven Seraphine yet for letting me suffer as an immortal. I might forgive her if she tells me she would have given it to me if Sarah had died last year."

Toussaint was not liking where the conversation was going. "Where are the bottles now?" He didn't want him to make a rash decision before he and Ivy had a chance to help them fix it.

"Seraphine took them with her. She showed up here, tore our lives apart, then took her *gift* and left again."

Now that Adam was talking in English again and seemed open to talking, Toussaint took a chance. "What happened after I left? You guys couldn't agree on which potion to take?"

Adam leaned forward, the scars across his face shining with the force of his emotion. "I didn't get a say. Sarah wouldn't take the potion to become immortal because Seraphine said Alex wasn't allowed to take it. She wouldn't let me take the potion to be mortal because she said she wouldn't give me a death sentence." He flung himself back against the couch. "She didn't care that I said I wanted to grow old with her. She couldn't ask me to die for her, and she couldn't change without her son, so she just took off."

Toussaint was stunned speechless. He hadn't thought of it like that but in a way, Adam becoming mortal was a death sentence. He respected her reasons; however, he had enough faith in Seraphine to know that Alex was going to be okay. Seraphine always had a plan, and there was no way she would let the boy grow old and die while his mother stayed young forever.

Now how did he help Ivy fix the issue when she knew nothing of immortals?

His savior chose that moment to knock on the apartment door. Toussaint answered it to find Penny and Asald standing on the other side. By the smiles on their faces, they must not be up to date on the drama.

Penny picked up the vibe first. "What's wrong?"

She rushed past him and stopped as she caught sight of Adam on the couch, eating the cake. Toussaint thought putting it on the coffee table was safe, apparently not.

Asald rested a hand on Toussaint's shoulder. "You don't look so good and he," he pointed at Adam, "looks like he's been run over by a truck a few times."

Adam saved Toussaint from trying to figure out how to word what happened delicately. "Seraphine swooped in, offered us an impossible deal, Sarah took Alex and left. No more wedding, sorry you made the trip out here." He mumbled as if he was still drunk.

Toussaint walked over to the kitchen table and sat down. He rested his throbbing head in his hands and waited for the barrage of questions he knew was coming.

Penny's training as a social worker kicked in. She grabbed the cake and handed it to Asald then walked over and quietly sat next to Toussaint. "Please tell me you can make more sense of that and you know where they are?"

Toussaint kept his voice low, he didn't want to trigger Adam. He recapped Seraphine's visit, the choice, and Sarah's refusal to let either of them take a potion. "I was downstairs with Ivy when Sarah came down and told her to pack up and leave. Ivy texted me they are at a motel an hour outside of town. She's going to try to talk to Sarah but you and I both know she can't help because she doesn't know the truth of the town."

Penny stood and walked over to Asald, who was discreetly dipping his fingers in the frosting and eating it. "I'm going to her, I can help. You need to stay here and fix all this." She waved her arm in a large circle indicating the trainwrecks that were Adam and Toussaint.

He leaned down and kissed her before addressing the room at large. "What are we doing about the rehearsal tonight?"

Adam grabbed the small pillow off the couch and covered his face.

Toussaint stared daggers at him for being so callous in front of Adam.

Penny was the patient one. "Give me a couple of hours then I'll text you with a plan. This was supposed to be Sarah's *Happily Ever After* and damn it if we're not getting it for her."

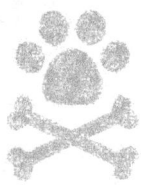

Seventeen

Ivy carried the to-go container of pancakes back to their room. Sarah looked a little better when she woke up but didn't feel up to going out in public yet. Alex was taking it all in stride, Ivy teared up any time he went over and tucked her in or asked her if she needed anything.

She was surprised when they went into the room and heard the shower running.

A noise behind her had her spinning back towards the parking lot. "Hey, you guys are back." Penny stood there with a bucket of ice. "Toussaint told me what happened, so I got here as fast as I could."

Ivy stepped aside and let her in. "How did you get her out of bed?"

Penny glanced down at Alex then walked a few feet away. "She had a good cry, I let her vent for a few minutes then I told her she stunk and needed to clean up. I got a small smile out of her then she went and did as I asked." Penny shrugged as if it was nothing when Ivy had been trying since yesterday to snap her out of her catatonic state.

Ivy set the container of food on the nightstand and sat on the edge of the bed. "So, did she tell you what happened?"

The lines around Penny's eyes tensed, she nibbled her lower lip. "She told me a little. I think I have her convinced to at least go back and talk to Adam." She lowered her voice when the water shut off. "I think it was just an automatic response to run and she realizes she needs to go work it out."

As the bathroom door opened, Ivy scooted back to the headboard and cuddled the pillow on her lap. She watched Sarah come out with one towel wrapped around her body and another one twisted around her hair. "Hey there, you're looking better. We brought you some pancakes."

Alex ran up and gave her the container of food.

Sarah bent and kissed the top of his head. 'Thank you, baby." She took the food over to the small table in front of the window and started eating.

Everyone stared at her, no one knew what to say next. Ivy's phone buzzed in her pocket, she pulled it out and saw a text from Toussaint.

Toussaint: Heads up, Penny is on her way there to help.

Ivy: A little late, she's been here a while and already got Sarah to do more than I managed to do since we left. Not that I'm jealous, I'm all for anything that gets her back to town. How's Adam?

Toussaint: We're hungover, and thanks to Adam, we need another cake for the rehearsal dinner if it's still happening.

Ivy: I think we're going to head back in a couple of hours. I'll keep you posted.

Sarah closed the lid after she finished eating and turned to glance between Penny and Ivy. "So, you think I should go back?"

Penny spoke first. "You know my vote. I saw Adam this morning, and it wasn't a pretty picture. That boy is destroyed, and I've been through enough with you to say honestly he deserves more and you need to go back and fix this."

Ivy was surprised by Penny's bluntness, but she had been there every day helping Sarah when she finally left Hank for good, and she's the one who protected Alex when Hank showed up and attacked them at the shelter. That probably afforded her the luxury of being blunt when she wanted to be.

Sarah turned to Ivy to hear her opinion.

"You know I had reservations about this from the beginning. Now that I've met him and I've seen him with you and Alex I have no doubt you are exactly where you're supposed to be."

Sarah glanced over at Alex and smiled as he sat on the floor playing with Zeus. "I'll go talk to Adam, but I'm not promising the wedding is still on."

Ivy's shoulders dropped in relief. "Let me shower, then we can go." She grabbed her phone, her duffel bag of clothes, and went into the bathroom. She was so relieved they were heading back she texted Toussaint.

Ivy: Penny is a miracle worker, we're heading back soon. I'm not sure the rehearsal dinner is going to happen though. See you soon.

Toussaint: Thank God, any more time with Adam and I may slit my wrists.

Ivy: While Adam and Sarah are talking, I'll buy you a drink.

Toussaint: Ugh, don't talk about drinking, I may throw up.

Ivy: How about lunch instead?

Toussaint: Sounds like a plan, see you soon.

Ivy set her phone on the counter and smiled at herself in the mirror. Maybe she had a shot after all but did she want something with him? She didn't want a long distance relationship, and she couldn't imagine picking up and moving for a guy. Relationships were messy as evidenced by their current motel situation but what about a casual hook up? Would he be willing to be her fuck buddy for a few days or would one of them get too attached?

Eighteen

Toussaint had never been a father, but taking care of broken-hearted men had become a specialty for him. When his brother lost his mate, Toussaint literally had to pick him up off the floor and take care of him for weeks before the grief had subsided enough that he could start taking care of himself again.

Now he was in the same boat with Adam. Asald and Toussaint finally managed to get him up and showered but hadn't told him yet Sarah was on her way back. He thought Sarah should see what a wreck Adam was. Anything he could do to help stir their emotions and get them talking is what they needed if the wedding was going to happen the next day. When the girls got back, they were going to have to decide what to do about the rehearsal dinner.

It didn't take long for news to spread in their town, so his phone had been blowing up all morning. Everyone loved Sarah and Adam and wanted to help any way they could. Unfortunately, there wasn't anything anyone could do.

Finally, the text he had been waiting for came in, Ivy and the girls were in the parking lot and coming up. "Hey, Adam, we're going to be right back. Asald and I need to check on something outside."

Adam was sitting at the kitchen table mindlessly adjusting the various decorations. Toussaint took that as a good sign that he may still think there was hope. The sullen man simply nodded and continued fiddling with the flowers.

They left the apartment and made it one floor down before they ran into the girls. Sarah smiled shyly at them but kept walking up to her apartment.

Asald grabbed Penny around the waist and pulled her in for a deep kiss. Toussaint was pretty sure they'd only been apart a few hours, so the spectacle was mildly nauseating. Then again they had only been together two years, so they were still in that honeymoon phase.

Alex giggled as he watched them, Ivy looked at Toussaint, rolled her eyes and chuckled. "I feel like we should shake hands or something."

Toussaint glanced down at her lips for a brief second. "A fist bump seems a little more personal than a handshake." He held his fist up like a complete idiot and waited for her to do the same.

Alex reached up, and fist bumped him instead.

Toussaint looked at Ivy and shrugged then bent down, so he was eye to eye with the boy. "Thanks, little man. Should we go get some lunch?"

Penny interrupted, "Actually, how about Asald and I take Alex for a while, and you guys grab lunch."

Her attempt at matchmaking wasn't going unnoticed by anyone.

Alex reached up and patted Ivy's arm. "Can I take Zeus with me?"

If Toussaint didn't know better, he would think the kid was in on the matchmaking too.

Ivy set the dog down. "Sure, but this time you can't let him out of your sight, okay?"

Penny grabbed Asald's hand and started dragging him down the stairs. "You two have fun now."

Once they were gone, the tension ramped up. Toussaint couldn't blame the other couple, they didn't know about his vow to avoid love which was reaffirmed after all the drama the last forty-eight hours.

Ivy clasped her hands in front of her and bounced on the balls of her feet. "We don't have to have lunch if you don't want to. I'm a big girl and can entertain myself."

Toussaint was torn but being a gentleman won out. "I think we both deserve a break after what we just went through. We could go to the

Fireside Grill if you want? It's not a bad walk, or we can drive if you prefer?"

"I'm good for a walk, let's go."

They only made it a block before Ivy's attention was caught. "What's going on over there?"

Toussaint glanced to the right and saw a large group of people around the gazebo that was in the center of town. "Everyone refuses to believe the wedding is off, so they are still setting it up as if it were happening."

They took a short detour to see the progress. Seraphine stood in the center of the gazebo with a clipboard in her hand. As fast as people came up and asked what was next, she sent them on their missions. She spotted Toussaint and Ivy and walked to meet them.

The older woman studied their faces for a second before saying anything. "Is she back?"

Toussaint waved at Saroj who was balancing on a ladder trying to hang a string of lights up. "She returned about twenty minutes ago, we left them in the apartment talking."

Ivy sighed heavily, "She doesn't know yet if the wedding is still going to happen."

Seraphine stared off in the distance before addressing them again. "Everything will be fine. She doesn't know me very well, so I'm not offended that she doesn't trust me." She stared down at her clipboard again before continuing. "Adam will help her, I don't think we'll see them tonight, but the wedding will still happen. I'll let Meddie know you will be there for your hair appointments in the morning."

Per her usual eccentric behavior, she forgot about them and went back to preparing for the wedding.

Toussaint was used to it, but Ivy was still trying to figure everyone out. "Penny swears she is all there, I'm not convinced though. My grandma acted a lot like her just before dementia took over.

Toussaint rested his hand gently on her lower back and guided her back on the sidewalk towards the restaurant. "I've known Seraphine longer than I care to admit. Trust me, she has more mental clarity than all of us combined. She's just an eccentric woman."

Ivy moaned, "Oh my god, what is that smell? My mouth is watering."

Toussaint's mind immediately went into the gutter thinking about her mouth watering but recovered quickly. "I think you are smelling Alizon's candy store. I smell sugar, and as we get closer, you'll start tasting it in the air too. I don't know how she does it, but I'm okay with it."

Ivy paused at the window of the store and gawked at all of the chocolates and candies on display. "I don't care how full I am we're stopping here on the way back. I need all of this in my life."

Toussaint didn't blame her, he stopped at the store way more often than he cared to admit. "Well, let's get you food than."

His hand naturally found its way to her lower back again. His mind needed to tell the rest of his body that he wasn't interested.

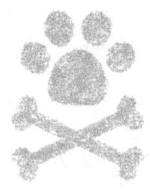

Nineteen

The Fireside Grill was as impressive as the rest of the town. Ivy loved the fire theme and wanted to know where she could get her own corset with large scales on it. It screamed *I'm a sexy bitch* and you can't touch me. Ivy's favorite foreplay was to tease a guy until he was begging for release.

A man slapping Toussaint on the back pulled her attention from the dirty thoughts she was enjoying. "My friend, how are things going? Are we having a wedding tomorrow?"

Ivy was surprised by his candidness. Was the entire town invested in Adam and Sarah's relationship?

Toussaint rubbed the back of his neck, "I wish I knew, but Seraphine is sure insistent it's still happening." He turned and waved towards Ivy. 'Pietr Drakki this is Ivy Grange, she is the Maid of Honor in tomorrow's ceremony." He waved his other hand towards Pietr. "And Pietr is the owner of this restaurant and cousin to Victoria who you met at the shower yesterday."

Ivy reached and shook his hand. He was much smaller than Toussaint, his dark features gave him a look of mystery. Ivy found him attractive, but he didn't hold a candle to Toussaint. She liked her men big and tall, and he fit the bill perfectly.

"Would you like a table in the backroom?" Pietr winked at Toussaint. Ivy guessed he was offering them privacy, which she didn't mind at all.

Toussaint held his hand up and shook his head. "We're just friends, any table works but you know I don't like sitting in the middle of the room."

Pietr waved them forward. "Follow me to my finest corner table."

Once they were sat, Ivy studied the menu for a minute before setting it down and sitting back in her chair. Before she could strike up a conversation, the waitress was greeting them.

"Hi, my name is Daphne, I'll be your server today. What can I get you?"

Toussaint looked to Ivy to order first. "I'll have a coke and a chicken Caesar salad please."

Toussaint quirked an eyebrow at her. "I'm all for a good salad, but this place is known for how well they grill their meat. It's your choice, however, I encourage you to try something else."

Ivy picked up the menu and studied it for a second. She wasn't terribly hungry, but now she felt like she had to try something else. "Okay, how about a cheeseburger medium with cheddar cheese."

Toussaint nodded and set his own menu down. "I'll have whatever is on draft and a sirloin medium rare with french fries."

Once they were alone again, Ivy studied the man across from her. "So, are you a Black Hollow native?"

Toussaint took the silverware out of his napkin and laid it across his lap. "Pascal and I came over here from France a long time ago. We traveled around a bit before finding Black Hollow and settling down. What about you, where are you from?"

"I grew up in Chicago, after college, I started a low-level job at an advertising firm, and now I'm an account manager. I like the creative outlet, it keeps me from getting bored."

Toussaint nodded. "I know exactly what you mean. Pascal and I started out as builders then got the bug for actually designing unique buildings and have slowly been working on one business at a time and bringing them out of the drab eighteen hundred aesthetic."

Ivy's jaw dropped. "You and your brother designed Scales 'N Tails and The Rotten Meatball? They are so unique inside. If you let me do a few advertising campaigns for the town, I could have tourists flocking here."

Toussaint's mouth opened and closed a couple of times before speaking. "I think we're all pretty happy with the quiet, small-town feel here. We don't mind a few tourists now and then, but for the most part, we like keeping to ourselves and knowing everyone around us."

Ivy thought that sounded lonely and depressing, but who was she to tell them how to live their life?

Ivy was never one to be shy or beat around the bush, so she charged on. "You've got to be what, thirty-five? Ever been married?"

She definitely shocked him with that one. He studied the table for a minute then shocked her right back. "I should probably be upfront with you right now. I have no interest in a relationship, and I'm definitely not the marrying kind."

She laughed at how flustered he was. "Relax big guy, I was just curious about you. I'm not looking to tie you down, well maybe in a casual way if you want." She paused as the waitress set down their drinks then left again. "I'm just here for a wedding, then I'll be gone."

Before the conversation could get any more

uncomfortable, their phones buzzed at the same time. Ivy picked hers up and saw it was a group text from Penny.

Penny: I haven't heard from Sarah. I refuse to accept this is over. Let's still have the rehearsal tonight, so at least the rest of us know what the hell we're doing tomorrow.

Another text came in almost immediately.

Asald: Let's be honest; it's about the food. We can't cancel the dinner now so we might as well feast."

Ivy rolled her eyes; typical guy just cares about the food. She sent a text back.

Ivy: Way to be compassionate there Asald. I'm good for a run through, see everyone at 6 p.m. at the gazebo.

Ivy shook her head. "You guys are the most determined bunch I've ever met. I'd hate to see what you guys would do if they were really resisting."

Toussaint shrugged, "It's what you do for friends."

Ivy's heart melted, the men of Black Hollow all seemed like tough guys, but they were really romantics at heart. Toussaint's vow to remain single was a shame, she thought he had the potential to be a perfect husband.

Twenty

Seraphine stood on the top step of the gazebo, clipboard in hand, looking like she was ready to do battle.

Toussaint didn't remember anyone appointing her as the official wedding coordinator, but maybe it was helping her guilty conscious with all the drama her choice caused.

She stood silently as everyone gathered, laughter filtered through the group as they caught sight of Saroj coming out of his ice cream store. He was in a full tuxedo, every strand of hair on his body perfectly combed.

Seraphine didn't laugh. Toussaint could see her fighting to not smile. "Saroj you are looking rather dapper this evening."

The yeti threw his arms up, gesturing at the rest of the group. "I thought we were rehearsing for tomorrow. Why is no one dressed?"

Cade ever the one to focus on fashion chimed in. "You're right, we really should have. You look like a million bucks while the rest of us are in rags."

Murmurs went around the group, everyone defending their wardrobe choice.

Seraphine cleared her throat and waited till all eyes were on her. "Thank you all for coming, I know this seems strange but given it's been a really long time since we've had a wedding. I think it best we have a run through." She glanced at her paper and looked back up. "Mayor Latsis you will join me up here as you are the officiant. Derrick and Raveena have agreed to play the parts of Adam and Sarah." Adam and the Mayor walked up the steps. Ivy was shocked at the Mayor's appearance. He looked like he had a lion's mane. She couldn't tell where his hair stopped, and his facial hair started.

Seraphine continued on. "Saroj you will be walking Sarah down the aisle." She waved at the yeti to take Raveena to the back of the group. "In order of coming down the aisle, Alizon and Aristide, you will go first followed by Nerissa and Pascal. Next is Silver and Cade, have you decided which of you is on the ladies' side?"

Silver stepped forward. "We decided since Cade has known Adam the longest he would stand on his side. That means I get to be one of the sexy ladies."

The group chuckled. Toussaint was glad to see how much Silver had come out of his shell since moving to Black Hollow and getting together with Cade. Even more impressive was how Silver was able to get Cade to slow down working and enjoy life. They used to go weeks without seeing him outside of his studio, and now they see him around town a few nights a week.

Seraphine interrupted his musings. "Penny and Ivy, you are co Maid and Matron of Honor. What order have you decided on?"

The two women exchanged glances and shrugged. Toussaint hoped Penny asked to go last, he felt awkward being the Best Man.

Penny chose for them. "Honestly, we hadn't asked Sarah because we were both fine with however she wanted it. I'll go with Silver's logic since Toussaint has known Adam longer they can go last."

Ivy didn't notice Toussaint giving her the side eye. He had hoped he would be walking with her but until now wasn't sure. He wondered how she felt about being the head of the line, was she dreading it like he was?

Seraphine made a note then looked up at the group. "Well, what are you waiting for. Get in your positions." She glanced down to Alex, who had been sitting in the grass, silently entertaining Zeus. "You are the ring bearer, so you need to go back with Raveena."

He hopped up and ran to catch up to the group. The wedding party made their way over to Saroj's ice cream shop and went inside. They weren't getting married in a church, and Adam didn't want to see Sarah until she was coming down the aisle so this was the best they could come up with.

Everyone lined up in order. Alizon and Aristide were about to step outside when Saroj told them to hold on. Toussaint watched as he went over to an outlet and plugged in two long extension cords. The outside of the store lit up. Saroj had strung wire from his store to the front of the gazebo and crisscrossed strands of lights all the way across creating a tunnel from the door of his shop to where they will stand to get married.

Toussaint glanced down when he heard Ivy gasp next to him. Her hand covered her mouth, her eyes shone bright with tears.

Penny walked over and hugged Saroj. "This is truly amazing, Sarah is going to love it."

Saroj's face turned red, strange to see the yeti so embarrassed. "I know a little of her past, and I wanted to make sure she had a special day."

Much to the surprise of the yeti, the women of the bridal party surrounded him and gave him a group hug. Toussaint was mildly jealous, he wanted to be surrounded by gorgeous women.

Ivy stepped away and came back over to Toussaint's side. "The more I get to know everyone here, the more I get how special it is and why you don't want a lot of tourists invading."

Toussaint wondered if she would feel the same way if she knew the truth of their paranormal town.

Alizon leaned over and got his attention. "Why isn't Sebastian here? I'm surprised he's not in the wedding."

Toussaint glanced down at Ivy, trying to figure out how to explain without Ivy questioning it. "He thinks some of the more unique citizens might get a little crazy at the reception, so he wanted to be on duty."

Alizon nodded. "Good idea, I hadn't thought of that."

A loud whistle from outside got everyone's attention. Mayor Latsis waved at them to start.

Everyone got in order, a recording of music started playing from somewhere outside.

Alizon and Aristide linked arms and began the walk down the aisle.

When it was their turn, Ivy held her arm out and waited for him to offer his. Goosebumps ran along his skin as soon as her hand touched him. A faint buzz of electricity coursed through his body. He groaned...that was not a good sign. If his body was trying to tell him she was his mate, he was going to be really pissed.

As the wedding party lined up on the steps of the gazebo, they watched as Alex and Zeus made their way down followed by Saroj looking like a proud papa escorting Raveena. He did realize it was only pretend and Raveena wasn't the bride, right?

Toussaint glanced up and was overwhelmed with the emotions he saw on Derrick's face. The man was utterly enraptured, it was apparent he was completely enamored with her. It was rare to see men cry, but there was definitely a slight sheen in Derrick's eyes. Toussaint glanced over at Ivy, maybe finding his mate wasn't such a bad thing after all.

Twenty-One

Ivy's alarm went off at eight a.m., they should be getting ready for the wedding right now. Instead, she was waiting with bated breath for Sarah to tell her what was happening.

Once the rehearsal was over last night, the group walked to Scales 'N Tails for dinner. Nerissa's brother Tristan had prepared an incredible buffet of food.

When Ivy had eaten there a few days earlier, she hadn't met the brother. Now that she saw him, she was resisting the urge to fan herself. He had a thick mane of wavy blonde hair and bright green eyes. The muscles of his arms bulged as he carried the trays of food out.

Ivy had been treated as one of the group, they laughed, drank wine, and took bets on who the next wedding in town was going to be.

After dinner, she had hoped Toussaint was going to come home with her, but after walking her home, he waited while she went inside the apartment then left.

Frustrated with being so close to such raw masculinity all day she was on edge and needing release. She was in town for a wedding, so she hadn't packed a vibrator. To her relief, she remembered there was a handheld showerhead. The previous tenant must have been a single woman.

Sarah had finally answered her texts and said she and Adam were still talking and not to worry. If there was a problem, Ivy knew Sarah would have been able to signal her. She fell asleep confident everything was going to work out.

The sun peeking through the curtains was blinding. Hating mornings as she did, she flopped over and faced the wall instead of getting up and getting ready. As she started to doze off her phone buzzed. It was a group text with Sarah and Penny.

Sarah: The wedding is on. I'll be downstairs in thirty minutes so we can walk over to Meddie's. Penny, thank you for keeping Alex!

Ivy punched the air as she shouted with excitement. She was a naturally optimistic person, but even she had been a little unsure it was going to happen.

Penny: I knew you guys would work it out, see you soon.

Ivy backed out of that message and went to her chat with Toussaint.

Ivy: Spread the word, the wedding is on! See you soon.

Toussaint: Seraphine's never going to let it go that she was right again. I'll spread the word.

Ivy grabbed Zeus and held him up to her face. "I'm not the only one getting gussied up today. The pet store does grooming, I know you don't like it, but my wedding date needs to be handsome." The dog looked at her and blinked. "Let's take you out then I need to shower."

After a quick trip downstairs, she jumped in the shower and tossed on a loose sundress. She still didn't know what their dresses looked like for the wedding. She had been told to send her measurements then found out the other day that Cade was the one making their outfits. It was guaranteed to be the fanciest article of clothing she likely ever owned. A custom-made dress by one of the country's hottest designers was a dream come true. She hoped it was the kind that could be worn again.

She slipped on her sandals at the same time Sarah knocked on the door. She grabbed her duffle bag and walked out. She studied her cousin for a few seconds, she physically looked fine. Of course, she was too beautiful to even have puffy eyes. "Are you good?"

Sarah reached out and pulled her into a hug. "I'm sorry I panicked, an old habit, I guess.

Thank you for not pushing me and taking off with me without notice."

Ivy pulled back and rested her hands-on Sarah's face forcing her to look at her. "I will always be there for you, no matter what. Don't ever apologize for taking care of yourself."

Sarah nodded, tears in her eyes she whispered. "I'm getting married today to the most amazing man."

Ivy pulled her back into a hug. "Yes, you are."

"I messed everything up, is anyone even going to show up?" Sarah mumbled.

Ivy squeezed her. "In my short time here, I've come to truly appreciate your new friends. I have no doubt everything will work out. Now, let's go get you ready. And by the way, one day soon I hope you'll tell me what all that was about."

Sarah winked at her. "I have a feeling I'll be able to tell you soon, and you'll understand."

They walked the short distance to Meddie's salon. Ivy covered Sarah's eyes the few feet they had to walk within view of the gazebo. She didn't want Sarah to know what the town had done for her yet.

The door of the salon swung open, they were pulled inside by giggling, excited women. Everyone was talking at once; apparently, Ivy wasn't the only one who had an ounce of doubt whether the wedding was going to happen.

Cade and Silver walked in behind them, pushing a clothing rack of dresses in bags. Cade grabbed the first bag and held it up for Alizon. "Sarah went for various shades of blue, so you each have similar dresses, but they will be slightly off from each other. The silk came from Astria, so it's going to hug you in all the right places."

Silver grabbed Nerissa's bag and handed it to her. "He's not even telling you the best part. There are small clips around the waist so right now they are long dresses. For the reception, you can hook them, and they turn into short dresses. Similar to how wedding dresses get bustled, but these hang smoothly."

Cade elbowed him. "Look at you using *bustled*, you're learning the lingo. Maybe I'll make you into an apprentice."

Silver's unexphand wrapped around Cade's neck so he could pull him close. "If it means spending more time with you, I'll do whatever you ask." He leaned in and kissed him deeply.

Ivy fanned herself this time, that was hot, and looking around she wasn't the only one who thought so.

Cade cleared his throat. "On that note, I'm heading back to my shop. The guys are getting dressed over there, and if I leave it up to them, they'll probably put something on backward or out of order. He gave Silver a quick peck on the lips and left.

Meddie stepped in the middle of the group. "No getting dressed until after your hair and makeup is done. Astria will kill me if any hairspray gets on her silk." She pointed to a rack of shirts hanging in the corner. "If you don't have something that you can easily slip down your body, then switch to a button-down shirt."

Ivy was glad she thought to wear the sundress, she only had to flick the spaghetti straps off her shoulders, and it would pool at her ankles.

Meddie pointed at her. "You have the least amount of hair, so you're going first, followed by Penny. That way by the time we need to get Sarah in her dress, you'll be ready to help."

The bell above the door rang as a woman walked in carrying a couple of boxes. Ivy couldn't help staring, she had thought the sun was glowing behind her, but once she was inside the glow was still there. "Sorry I'm late, we were up all night decorating the wedding cake, so I got a little distracted."

Penny grabbed one of the boxes and followed her over to a table in the sitting area. "Braelyn, have you met Ivy yet? She is Sarah's cousin." Penny waved towards the woman. "Braelyn is one of the bakers at Magical Delights Bakery."

The ethereal woman walked over and held her hand out. Ivy was almost to stunned by her beauty to move. "It's very nice to meet you, Ivy. You'll have to stop in and have a treat before you leave town."

Ivy snapped out of her daze. "Actually, Toussaint brought me some cinnamon rolls the other day. They were incredible, I definitely want more before I go."

Braelyn blushed, Ivy wouldn't have thought her to be so humble. She turned and walked over to Sarah. "I know today is going to get crazy, and I don't want you to forget to eat, so I brought a bunch of pastries, so I expect all of you to make sure she is taken care of." She made her way to the door and looked back one last time. "You're all going to look gorgeous today, have fun."

Ivy wasn't shy, as soon as the door closed, she made a beeline for the phenomenal smelling breakfast items. The rest of the group may be offended if she took a bite of every type of pastry inside so she grabbed a slice of cinnamon crumb bread and made her way to the chair in front of Meddie's station.

The young girl ran her fingers through Ivy's short blonde bob. "Did you give any thought to me adding extensions? I can match your color or give you some colored ones?"

Ivy glanced at Sarah in the mirror. "It's your day, what do you think?"

Sarah turned her head and studied her for a second. She walked over to the rack of dresses and glanced at Ivy's. "Her dress looks like it's cornflower blue, you think you can match that?"

Meddie rested her hands on her hips and gave her an exasperated look. "I can match any color Cade tries to throw at me."

Sarah smiled. "Let's do it."

Meddie nodded and went to the back room. Ivy was slightly scared, but it was only hair, and it was Sarah's day, so she was happy to oblige the bride. After all, how many times does your favorite cousin get married...to a good guy?

Twenty-Two

Toussaint sat on a couch in Cade's studio, waiting for the rest of the group to show up. Saoirse came out with a cup of coffee and handed it to him. "I have a whole pot ready to go. Cade and Silver are dropping the dresses off to Meddie's, and then they'll be back."

The doorbell rang as the door swung open, the rest of the groomsmen made their way inside, followed by Cade. Saoirse passed cups of coffee to everyone as Adam came in.

Toussaint thought he looked a little rough around the edges. "There's the man of the day. Are you ready for this?"

Adam yawned before collapsing onto the couch next to him. "I've maybe had four hours of sleep in two days. I don't care if you have to strap me to a gurney, you will get me down the aisle so I can marry her before she changes her mind again."

Pascal slapped him on the knee, "You need to keep your energy up, you need to be able to take care of business tonight."

Aristide ever the serious one sat down next to him. "Is she okay? You guys worked everything out?"

Adam accepted a cup of coffee from Saoirse and sat up. "I don't know how much you guys already heard, but Seraphine gave us a choice. She could make Sarah Immortal like me, or she could make me mortal so I can grow old with Sarah."

Toussaint glanced around, everyone stared at Adam in stunned silence.

"Sarah didn't want me to be mortal because she thought she was sentencing me to death. On the other hand, she couldn't imagine becoming immortal and leaving Alex mortal."

Aristide leaned forward. "This sounds like the makings of a good book. What did you guys decide."

Toussaint quirked his eyebrow at Aristide. Leave it to the bookstore owner to be so callous.

"It took a while, but I finally convinced her to have more faith in Seraphine. She had told us Alex had his own path to take and she couldn't make him immortal right now as an eight-year-old boy." He chugged the last sips of coffee. "Those two have been through so much I don't blame her at all for panicking. I know in my gut Seraphine wouldn't do anything to hurt any of us."

Pascal looked ready to pull his hair out, "So, what did you choose?"

Adam sighed. "I've wanted to die more times than I can count. Now that I've found my reason for living, I never want it to end. Sarah has decided to become immortal."

Aristide's jaw dropped. Apparently, he wasn't expecting that.

Toussaint thought it was the right choice and apparently Asald agreed.

"I think you guys made the right decision. Unfortunately, you made me realize Penny, and I haven't discussed this, and we don't even know if Christian takes after me or not yet." He stared out the window for a few seconds before turning back to the group. "I guess before we leave we better go visit Seraphine.

Cade clapped his hands together, making everyone jump. "Enough of this sadness. Strip down to your underclothes and go have a seat in the back."

Toussaint shared a look with the rest of the group before they started stripping. One thing about paranormals, they weren't shy with their bodies.

Aristide made it to the back first and yelled out. "Is this really necessary?"

Cade smiled a wide toothy grin as the rest of the group took off to see what they were missing.

Toussaint couldn't help but laugh. Misha and Vasily Rasputin stood next to a table full of grooming tools. Aristide was upset because the brother and sister owned the pet store and ran an annual pet wash in the center of town.

Cade walked back to join them. "If you think I'm letting you scrubs into my creations looking the way you do, you have another thing coming. You're all getting clipped, shaved, and combed so sit down and relax.

The group grumbled but did as they were told. Toussaint thought he did a good job getting ready this morning, but if he was going to stand next to the groom, maybe he ought to leave it to the professionals. He wasn't about to admit he wanted to look good for Ivy.

Twenty-Three

Ivy was in love, the dress Cade made was incredible. How he managed to make it a perfect fit when he hadn't even seen her body was a mystery to her. She felt silly doing it, but she couldn't resist twirling a few times in front of the mirror.

To bring the whole look together, Meddie had perfectly weaved blonde and blue extensions through her hair, so she had long curls flowing down her back. She hadn't had long hair since she was in middle school. She might have to consider growing it out.

Gasps around the room drew her attention away from the mirror. Sarah walked out, looking like perfection. Her silk dress was the same shiny silver as Adam's scars, Ivy thought it was going to look amazing next to him. The front and back both dipped into low V's with a thin piece of sheer cloth covered in crystals that caught the light and made her sparkle. She looked like a princess, and Ivy was sure Adam would treat her like one for the rest of their days.

Meddie walked out behind her and gave everyone a stern look. "Your makeup is perfect, no crying."

Penny choked on her tears. "Too late." She ran over and swallowed Sarah in a bear hug. Ivy understood exactly how Penny was feeling.

The bell above the door rang as Saroj came in looking as spiffy as he did the night before. "Ladies, it's almost that time. Is everyone ready?"

All eyes turned to Sarah and waited for her to nod.

Saroj walked towards the back of the salon. "Let's go through the back, so no one sees you all." He walked up to Sarah and bowed to her. "You look stunning, Adam is a lucky man."

Sarah reached up and kissed his cheek then turned and followed him out the back door.

When they got into the backroom of Saroj's ice cream shop, two tiny women were standing next to buckets of flowers. "Don't you all look gorgeous. Not that you need anything else to make you more perfect, but we do have all of your corsages and the boutonnieres for all the guys."

Ivy grabbed the bouquet being handed to her. Somehow, they had managed to have more shades of blue then Ivy had ever known was possible with flowers and laced silver ribbon throughout. It was a gorgeous effect and matched their outfits perfectly.

Sarah showed her bouquet off. "I love the rhinestones laced throughout, it is truly magical. Willa, Cora, you did a spectacular job."

The women blushed but didn't say anything else.

A loud noise from the front of Saroj's had everyone turning. The men of the wedding party came in boisterously until they caught sight of the women. Asald's entire face shifted, the look of lust and love he gave Penny was awe-inspiring. Ivy hoped one day she had someone look at her that way.

Asald walked up and hooked his hand around Penny's neck. "My god, how do you continue to grow more gorgeous every day?"

Alex ran over to Sarah. "Mommy, you look like a princess."

Sarah bent down and kissed his cheek. "And you are a dashing prince in your tuxedo."

He reached up and ran his hand through his slicked back hair. "Uncle Pascal says I'm going to have to beat the ladies back with a stick. I don't know why I would want to do that." He shrugged, clearly exasperated with the idea.

Sarah looked up and glared at Pascal who shrugged and tried to look innocent.

Cora handed a boutonniere to Ivy, she assumed it was for Toussaint. She hadn't looked at him yet, she didn't know why she was being a coward.

Finally, she glanced up and found him staring at her, there was heat in his eyes. She didn't know how to interpret it though. Her mouth went dry, he was fucking gorgeous. She was interested in him before but seeing him all suave and cleaned up her libido was in overdrive. She didn't care what she had to do, she was getting him in her bed before she left town.

He walked up and stopped in front of her. He ran his fingers through one of the long curls of her hair. "You look so different."

Ivy bit her lip, feeling unsure of herself. "We thought it would be a fun change for the day."

His hand came up and grabbed her chin, so she was forced to look into his eyes. "I think you were beautiful just the way you were."

Ivy was at a loss for words, his tone wasn't romantic, but his words sure were. Didn't every woman want a man who loved them as they were and not with all the social norms women were forced to endure?

Love? She didn't know where that word came from. "That's very sweet of you."

He stepped back and cleared his throat, he seemed as uncomfortable with the moment of intimacy as she was. She distracted them both by pinning the flowers on to his jacket.

Sebastian poked his head in the back room. "I have a delivery for Ivy. I think it's a dog, but I'm not totally sure."

Ivy rushed over and scooped Zeus out of his arms. "You look so good, they did a great job." They had given him a blue bow tie and combed his hair down. She loved her fluff ball, but this look was a fun change.

Sebastian stared at the creature like it was going to attack any minute. "Seraphine said it's time to start, everyone is ready to go."

Sarah's eyes grew wide. "Everyone? People came?"

Every single person in the room turned and gave her their most sardonic look. Ivy didn't know when Sarah was going to accept that she was loved by everyone that had the good fortune to meet her.

Saroj held his arm out to Sarah. "Thank you for the honor of letting me walk you down the aisle."

The group lined up in order and made their way to the front door. Sebastian plugged in the lights and gave Saroj a thumbs up. Music echoed around the plaza, and the group started walking.

Ivy wished she could see Sarah's face when she saw the tunnel Saroj had created, but she was going to be in front of her.

When it was her turn to go, she linked arms with Toussaint and ignored the tingle of electricity that ran down her arm. This was going to be a long day being so close to him and not getting to cop a feel.

Twenty-Four

Toussaint was relieved the ceremony was over. Everything had gone perfectly, and he would never admit it, but he did tear up during their vows. Ivy probably thought he was a creeper, she had to have caught him staring at least ten times. He couldn't help it, she was beautiful, and her dress teased just the right amount of skin to make him crazy.

They packed into as few cars as possible and drove to Seraphine's for the reception. It was the only place big enough to hold the entire town, and until he had seen them all gathered today, he didn't realize just how big the town had grown.

As they drove through the streets, it was strange to see every store closed down with signs saying they were at the wedding. Who knew one tiny human could bring the whole town together but after the scare last year where she was almost killed by a suspected intentional poisoning; everyone had rallied behind her and become her champion. That was the first time in many years there was a real crime, and it scared everyone.

Toussaint didn't know how Seraphine did it, but her gate minions didn't bother anyone as they drove through the gates. It probably helped that it was a long stream of cars coming in one after another.

The wedding party was driven around the back and let out in front of a garden. He was surprised to see Julian sitting on a bench holding a camera. Julian was a necromancer and the town's funeral director, Toussaint didn't realize he was also into photography.

His assistant Ella came out from the back of the house and took charge. Over the next thirty minutes, they were put into various positions and poses. Toussaint's cheeks were burning, he didn't think he or any of the other guys had smiled this much in their hundreds of years life.

Finally, it was declared the pictures were done, Seraphine stood at the back of her house smiling down on all of them. "Refreshments are ready, and dinner will be served soon. Let's introduce the new couple to the town."

The ballroom was filled to capacity, and the music was already pumping. Toussaint spied Sebastian standing at the entrance watching over the crowd, he looked slightly flustered.

Toussaint walked up and slapped him on the back affectionately. "How's it going?"

Sebastian looked around, probably making sure Ivy wasn't nearby. "I have a bad feeling things are going to get out of control fast. As insane as Seraphine's All Hallows Eve party are we've never had the entire town in attendance." He glanced around once more. "Are you prepared to give Ivy *the talk* if she does see something unexplainable?"

"Honestly, I think Penny and Sarah should have already told her the truth. She has to be the most oblivious person I know. I can't imagine how she is explaining some of our weirdness to herself."

Ella called out to the group. "Everyone's dress bustled?" She waited for the ladies to nod. "Line up, Johnny is going to announce you."

Toussaint walked back over to Ivy and held his arm out. "I'll warn you now, Johnny Star is our local entertainer, and he is quite flamboyant. You will be shocked by his costume changes too, he can make himself look like almost any entertainer." He was also a shapeshifter, but she didn't need to know that.

Ivy jumped as a booming voice reverberated around the room. "Who's ready to meet Mrs. and Mr. Sarah Hannigan." Murmurs spread through the room, "Hey now, I'm a feminist, and that's how we're doing it so zip it."

Toussaint shook his head, Johnny was quite the character.

Ivy was laughing. "I like him already."

The booming voice quieted everyone again. "Before we get to the lovely couple how about introductions for the wedding party starting with Aristide and Alizon.

When it was their turn, Ivy had to drag Toussaint down the steps to the center of the dance floor. He did his best to smile and have fun. That was until he saw the vampires leering Ivy's way. The second he could get away he was going to make sure they knew she was off limits.

"Everyone gather round, it's time for the first dance as a married couple."

Toussaint started to walk off the dance floor when he was pulled back by Ivy. "Sarah doesn't want to be the center of attention. She wants the whole wedding party dancing."

Toussaint glanced over to scowl at Sarah. Then he noticed the strain around her eyes. She really didn't like all the focus on her. "Fine."

He had been trying to avoid having Ivy in his arms, he should have known it wouldn't work. He tried to keep distance between them, but she pulled him in close, he could feel every inch of her pressed against him. Her scent engulfed him, blood rushed to multiple parts of his body. He had to keep fighting the mating urge he knew was building.

He focused on the wall just above her head until the song was over and he was able to escape.

As the last line of the song rang out, he grabbed her hand and dragged her off the floor. He didn't want to be a complete dick and leave her standing there alone. "Do you need a drink? I need a drink."

Sebastian's bartenders stood behind the bar, waiting for orders. "I'll have a whiskey neat, and she'll have..." He turned and waited for her to order.

"I'll have the same."

Her answer surprised him, he liked that she wasn't afraid of the hard stuff.

He gulped down the first drink and immediately signaled for a second.

Ivy stared at him, her cup halfway to her mouth. "Are you okay?"

He glanced her way, his eyes taking her in from head to toe before taking the second drink and gulping it down. "I'm not a fan of crowds, just trying to relax."

Pascal and Josephine walked up and joined them. Josephine smiled at Ivy. "The sign I made looks awesome in my house. That was a very cool idea."

"Awe, thanks. I couldn't have done it without Toussaint. He helped me cut and sand all the signs before the shower."

"That explains why you disappeared for an entire day," Pascal commented.

Josephine linked arms with Toussaint. "You look a little distressed, how about a dance."

He glanced over at Ivy, he didn't want to want her, but he didn't want to leave her either. She made the choice for him. "You guys go have fun, I'm going to go dance with this handsome hunk." She grabbed Pascal and pulled him out to the floor.

Toussaint wanted to growl and pound his chest and tell his brother to stay away. Instead, he smiled down at Josephine and escorted her out to the floor. He pulled her in his arms and went through the motions, but his eyes never left Ivy. He hated watching her laughing with his brother. Did she think Pascal was funnier? What if she liked him better? He shook his head at his pouting, what was he, fifteen?

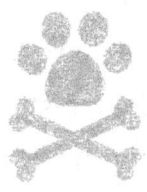

Twenty-Five

Ivy could tell Toussaint was affected by her, but he was fighting it. She understood that he wanted to be single. In her mind he was cutting his nose to spite his face. Who better to help her figure him out than his own twin brother.

As the dance started, she studied Pascal. She had to admit the similarities were startling, but Toussaint was a little thicker, a little sexier.

He obviously picked up on his brother's issues too. "So, you're the girl who has had my brother in knots for the last week. I admit, I never expected such a tiny thing could have so much control over him."

She scoffed. "You could have fooled me. He outright told me he was single and proud and nothing was going to change that. I've tried flirting, but he resists me at every turn. Yet he continues to hang around me, he's so confusing."

Pascal frowned at his brother across the dance floor. "I'm afraid that's my fault." He sighed heavily, Ivy was intrigued. "I lost my wife a few years ago. I wasn't strong, I almost didn't survive the loss. He saved my life, but it took a toll on him. He's afraid of love, afraid of loss. It took me a long time to live again, and I'll be honest, I hope I find love again. I don't know that he will ever be able to open his heart and take a chance. He might be a lost cause."

Ivy's heart broke for both of them. She couldn't imagine losing a spouse or almost losing a sibling, but he deserved happiness too.

"On a brighter note, can we talk about that animal you brought with you. What the hell is it?"

Ivy threw her head back and laughed. She loved people's reactions to Zeus, they just didn't recognize perfection when they saw it.

***

Ivy's feet were killing her. She had ditched her heels right after the cake was cut, but she hadn't stopped dancing since and her body was begging her to stop.

She found Penny and Asald standing with Sarah and Adam and made her way towards them. "Quick question, where is Alex going tonight?"

Sarah and Adam looked at each other, then back at her. Sarah shrugged, "Home with us?"

Ivy wasn't having that. "I refuse. He can stay with me. Zeus likes cuddling with him anyways."

Penny stared at something over her shoulder for a second before jumping in. "I don't think your night is going to be over any time soon."

Ivy turned and gasped. Toussaint was leaning against the wall, his legs were crossed, hands in his pockets, his eyes hooded as he stared at her. He was radiating sexual tension, and Ivy felt the need instantly explode in front of her. "Crap."

"What's that?" Penny asked with a big smile on her face.

Ivy turned back towards the group. "I might need to call an Uber and get out of here."

She didn't act fast enough, all eyes were on something behind her, and their smiles were growing bigger by the second.

Hot breath tickled her ear as someone leaned in and whispered. "You look good enough to eat."

Ivy's knees buckled slightly. She'd been wanting him to show interest in her, and he went from zero to sixty in no time. That one small sentence had her growing wet instantly. She wasn't going to let him win that easily, he had kept her at arm's length all week.

She turned her head slightly and looked over her shoulder at him. "I'm sure there is someone around here who can help me with that. I met some nice guys over by the bar earlier, maybe I'll go find them."

He growled in her ear, goosebumps ran down her arms.

Penny choked back a laugh. "Asald, I think Alex needs to go to bed, and you need to talk to me like he is talking to her right now." She kissed Sarah on the cheek, grabbed her husband's hand, and dragged him away.

Ivy started to feel slightly panicked that she had poked the bear and wouldn't be strong enough to handle him, and her friends were deserting her.

Sarah grabbed Adam's hand. "I think it's time for us to leave too. Let's go say goodbye to Seraphine then you can show me how much you love me." She winked at Ivy and took off.

Ivy turned slowly and came face to face with Toussaint. "Can I take you home?"

She wasn't sure how innocent his question was, and she prayed he meant it in the naughtiest way possible. The problem was, they were too far to walk back to the apartments, and they didn't have their cars. "We should probably find a ride."

One side of his mouth curved up in a sexy grin. "I can fly us there, come on."

He grabbed her hand and pushed his way through the crowd. As they passed Pascal, she grabbed his hand and mouthed the word help.

He jumped in front of Toussaint and slowed him down. "Where's the fire?"

Toussaint tried to push past him but was held back. He leaned in to whisper to his brother. Ivy didn't think he realized he had no volume control when he was drunk. "I can't fight it any longer, I need her."

Pascal pushed back on his chest. "Maybe you should wait until your sober."

Ivy didn't dare laugh, but she was tempted when Toussaint's shoulders dropped in defeat, and he mumbled. "Fine."

"How about we make sure she gets home then you can sleep this off."

Ivy was relieved, she wasn't going to turn him away, she'd wanted him for too long. Although the sheer size of him was intimidating, and she wasn't sure she could have handled him in his current state. He's finally interested, and he probably won't remember tomorrow.

Twenty-Six

It had been at least two hundred years since Toussaint woke up hung over. And now, it's happened not only once but twice. His eyes felt like they had dirt in them as he opened them and tried to figure out where he was.

He was sitting on the floor in his bedroom, he had no memory of how he got there. He rolled over to push himself off the floor when pain shot through both his hands. He looked down, and the knuckles on both hands were shredded, his fingernails were dirty and torn. Ice cold fear ran through him. What had he done?

He finally made it to his feet and looked around his room, nothing seemed out of the ordinary. He vaguely remembered trying to take Ivy home; he prayed she was okay and had nothing to do with whatever happened to his hands.

His phone was nowhere to be seen, he went out to the living room and finally found it on the kitchen counter. It was three in the afternoon, he was really starting to panic about what happened. He hit the button to call his brother and paced while he waited for him to pick up. "Hey, you're alive."

"What happened last night?"

"I can catch you up later, I'm busy right now."

It was Sunday, Toussaint couldn't imagine what he was doing. "Where are you?"

"I'm at Saroj's, someone made a mess of the town last night. A bunch of us are out here cleaning up."

Dread washed over Toussaint, what were the odds he wasn't responsible for the destruction.

"Give me twenty, then I'll be there."

"Are you sure, you looked pretty out of it this morning when I peeked in on you."

"And you just left me on the floor?"

"You seemed comfortable to me," Pascal said defensively.

"Whatever, I'll shower and come over." He hung up without another word.

As quickly as he could without throwing up, he showered and drove through town. He couldn't believe his eyes as he passed by various businesses. The front window of Seren's apothecary was shattered, he could see entire shelves inside emptied of the bottles that were on there. It was the same scene at Alizon's candy store and much to his annoyance the giant ice cream cone he had built for Saroj was now shoved through his store window.

Toussaint felt sick to his stomach. He helped build all of these stores, there was no way he would be responsible for damaging them. He was going to go straight to the apartments to make sure Ivy was okay when he saw her come out of the ice cream parlor. She was covered in dust and carrying drywall out to a small dumpster Pascal must have brought over from their shop.

He parked and slid his hands in his pockets before walking over to the group. Everyone was somber, which was disappointing after how happy they had been the day before. "Do you guys know anything yet?"

Pascal shook his head. "Sebastian has been trying to take prints, but they are public places, he didn't think it would help much. He and a few of us his guys are going door to door and talking to everyone. He said most people are like you and still passed out from partying too hard last night.

Toussaint glanced over at Ivy, she smiled shyly before looking away.

Saroj came out of the shop, saw Toussaint, and rushed over. "I am so sorry about the cone, I know how hard you worked on it."

"As long as everyone is okay, it's nothing to stress over. I'll make you four more cones if you want."

Saroj's eyes lit up, Toussaint suddenly regretted his statement. "Let me grab some work gloves, and I'll help out."

He waited till he was alone at his truck before pulling his hands out and studying them. Could he really have done this?

Twenty-Seven

Ivy's muscles were sore, she wasn't out of shape, but she wasn't in shape either. After a night in high heels followed by a day of manual labor helping clean up around town, she seriously wanted a bath and her bed.

She shut off the water of the tub and was about to step into the water when someone knocked on her apartment door. She was sure she knew who it was. Toussaint had been trying to talk to her all day, but she had stayed busy and able to avoid him for the most part. It wasn't that she was mad at him. She was frustrated that it took a tank full of alcohol for him to realize he wanted her. Not that she had prospects banging down her door, but she had enough self-respect that she wasn't going to fall for a guy who wasn't completely into her.

She grabbed a towel and wrapped it around her body. She looked through the peephole and confirmed it was a contrite-looking Toussaint on the other side.

She opened the door, she heard him suck in his breath as he took in her lack of clothing. "I'm sorry, I should have asked if I could come over. I wanted to bring you these." He handed her a bouquet of flowers. "I don't remember much from last night. Pascal assured me I was a total ass and you deserve better than the way I treated you."

She stood back and held the door open. "Come in." She wasn't going to make this easy on him.

She sat on the couch and let the towel droop a little, she crossed her legs, letting a lot of thigh show.

He gulped loudly.

"Don't sweat it too much, you weren't truly horrible. I've been on worse dates."

He grimaced. "That isn't saying much for mankind."

She shrugged but didn't say anything else.

"Did you at least get home okay? I know some guys were watching you pretty closely."

She chuckled. "The only guy who I had to watch out for was you. But you and Pascal made sure I was safely home. I didn't think you should be climbing stairs in your state, but you were insistent in making sure I got in my door okay, which I thought was very sweet."

She left off the part where she was so sexually frustrated she had to take care of herself in the shower again.

Toussaint nodded then stood up. "Well, I'm sorry if I caused you any worry. I just wanted to make sure you were okay."

She resisted groaning, the wall was back up. She needed to find some alcohol stat to at least loosen him up a bit. She was about to stand up when she noticed his hands, she jumped up and grabbed them. "Oh my god, what happened?"

Toussaint didn't know what to say. How did he play it off, so she didn't get suspicious and connect it to what happened in town? "I think Pascal and I were messing around last night and I must have been a sloppy drunk."

"And you worked all day like this? Let me clean them." She went to the bathroom and came back with a small first aid kit. "Sit down."

She grabbed a bowl of warm soapy water and sat down on the coffee table across from him. She dipped a washcloth in the water then gently pressed it to each cut. He didn't say a word as she cleaned them, put ointment on them, and wrapped a couple of bandages around each hand.

She knew she was playing with fire, but as she finished, she lifted each hand to her mouth and kissed his palms. She didn't want to think anymore, she stood up and let the towel fall to the ground.

She enjoyed the look of shock on his face as she climbed up and straddled his lap. His hands laid limply next to him, he stared into her eyes. She could see he was fighting some internal war. The growing appendage she was straddling must have won out. Her skin burned as his fingers slowly trailed up her thighs and around her hips. He grabbed her ass and rocked her forward. Her eyes unfocused, she couldn't think as her clit hit the perfect spot on his jeans, causing an eruption of need through her body.

She had been planning to be the one in charge, she ended up being putty in his hands. He latched on to one of her nipples, his fingers dug into her ass cheeks as he rocked harder and faster until he finally ripped the orgasm from her.

Out of breath, she wanted to collapse against him, but he had other plans. He held onto her as he stood up and walked toward the bedroom. She wrapped her legs around his waist and kissed his neck as they went. Once he had to stop and hold on to the wall, he was quickly losing the ability to keep control, and Ivy loved it.

She wanted him to regret wasting the last week playing hard to get when they could have been doing this the whole time. He didn't know it yet, but she was going to fuck him into oblivion.

Twenty-Eight

Toussaint was torn in half, and it was making him crazy. He had gone over to the apartment to apologize for his behavior the night before, but somehow, he ended up in her bed buried deep inside her for most of the night.

He hadn't meant to cross the line; he knew if he could have just held out a little longer, she would have been gone and his heart would have been safe. As soon as she climbed onto his lap, he was a lost cause, and no force on Earth could have made him leave.

For as long as he could remember, he woke with the sun. He would give anything to sleep in once in a while, but his body just didn't cooperate. Today was the first day he didn't mind though. Ivy was curled against him, her head on his chest, quiet snores the only indication she was asleep.

They laid that way for a long time until their phones buzzed on the dresser. He probably would have ignored it but since both their phones went off and he was technically a criminal at large he figured he better get it and find out what was happening.

He slipped his arm out from under her and reached for his phone. It was a group text from Adam and Sarah saying they were leaving for their honeymoon and they were grateful to everyone who helped make their wedding perfect and especially to Penny and Asald for keeping Alex for a few days so they could be alone.

Toussaint rolled his eyes at some of the lewd comments being texted by Asald and Pascal. Those two were happy to give Adam advice on how to please his new wife.

Zeus laid at Toussaint's feet and flipped over to show his belly. "Are you needing some attention too?"

He scratched the mongrel for a minute then slipped on his pants. "How about I take you out, so your mommy doesn't need to get up."

The dog hopped up and ran circles around his feet. It had no qualms about potentially tripping him.

He sat on the bottom steps outside and let Zeus walk around the grass for a bit. A throbbing sensation started building in his hands. Glancing down he was still in shock at how damaged they were. All his years in construction had given him plenty of scars and calluses, this looked much more violent.

The throbbing intensified until his entire body felt like it was on fire. He tried to grab for the dog and get upstairs, his vision went black, and he hit the ground.

***

Toussaint and Zeus walked in the apartment and found Ivy standing at the kitchen counter pouring a glass of orange juice. "Thank you for taking him out, I appreciate it."

She walked over and handed him a glass of juice too. He looked at it but didn't take it. "We should talk."

He walked to the couch and sat down, he could see the confusion on her face as she walked over and sat next to him.

"I'm glad you woke up before I had to leave. It's been fun being with you, last night was entertaining, but we both have our own lives to get back to. Drive safe and let Penny and Sarah know you made it home."

He got up to leave. She grabbed his arm and tried to yank him down. "What the hell is happening?"

He shrugged, "We had a fling now you can go home."

Ivy's face turned red, her jaw clenched in anger as she spoke through gritted teeth. "You think it's okay to string me along all week, fuck me, then throw me away?"

He rolled his eyes. "Why are humans so dramatic. I told you I didn't want a relationship. You kept pushing. You were the one who offered a casual fling, I gave you what you wanted." He walked to the door and opened it, "I hope you enjoyed your visit to Black Hollow."

He didn't look back, just closed the door and went to work.

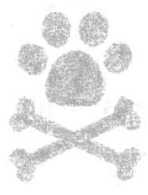

Twenty-Nine

Ivy was crushed, she had no preconceived notions that they were going to be a couple but to be rejected so coldly after being screwed was worse than anything she had experienced before.

She hated that she was crying, he didn't deserve her tears. He was right though, he repeatedly tried to keep a wall between them. She was stupid and kept pushing at it until he crumbled.

She marched around the apartment, anger fueling her. Zeus followed behind whining as she tossed things haphazardly into any bag or box she could find. With Herculean strength, she took everything to her car in two trips.

Zeus jumped into the passenger seat, she climbed behind the wheel and had to take a deep breath. She was shaking so hard she was afraid to drive.

Her cell phone buzzed in her pocket, it was a text from Penny.

Penny: We're going to get breakfast, want to meet us?

Ivy laughed bitterly.

Ivy: No thanks, I'm leaving town. Toussaint is an asshole, and I need to get far away from him. BTW...you may want to have the cops look into why his hands are all fucked up.

With more anger than necessary, she powered down the phone and tossed it on the seat with Zeus. She took one more deep breath to center herself then got out of town as fast as she could.

As the last buildings of the town disappeared from her rearview mirror, she relaxed a little in her chair and prayed the tears would stay away.

A shadow above the car had her glancing out her window. Something large was flying towards the car, it flew a few feet in front of her and landed in the road.

Ivy screamed, not a ladylike scream either. It was ear-piercing, and Zeus howled along with her even though he had no idea what was happening.

She slammed on the breaks, managing to miss the object by inches. She sat paralyzed as it came towards her. She had to be hallucinating, there was no other explanation as to why Toussaint was walking towards her with giant, black wings fluttering behind him. He tapped his knuckles on the window and gave her a bored look.

She cracked the window an inch but didn't say a word. He leaned down so only his eyes could be seen through the opening.

He sighed heavily. "I was told to let you go, then you went and told Penny to ask about my hands. Now Toussaint's friends are asking questions, and you have caused more trouble than you were worth."

Ivy wanted to throw up, it looked like Toussaint, but his voice was slightly different, and there was no life inside his eyes.

"We both know I can rip this door off the car and grab you, so why not save us both some trouble and come out."

Ivy didn't know what to do, fighting seemed like a bad idea. There was no guarantee she would fare any better if she cooperated. She glanced toward Zeus, hoping to grab her phone. Her heart sank seeing it on the floor, it must have flown off the seat when she slammed on the brakes.

"You can walk away right now, I'll keep going and won't come back here." She didn't know what was happening with Toussaint. She was scared and wanted to get far away without setting him off.

He wagged his finger back and forth. "I tried that already and you ratted me out. Now I need to make you pay, and since you told Penny you were leaving, and Sarah is on her honeymoon, that means I can take my time and enjoy myself."

Ivy wanted to scream, she wanted to cry, but she was no simpering victim. She was going to bide her time and find a way to escape.

He smiled as he reached for the door handle. "Be a good girl and move over. We have somewhere to be."

Thirty

Toussaint jerked awake, he didn't know how he had gotten back to his apartment. The last thing he remembered was taking Zeus out for a walk at Ivy's. Flashes of her crying and them in the woods kept popping up in his mind, and it made his blood run cold. He grabbed his cell phone off the bedside table and called her praying the entire time it was also some weird dream. He growled when it went right to voicemail. He sent a text asking her to call him when she had a minute.

He needed to see for himself that it was all in his head. He'd go to the apartment and find her there.

After a quick shower, he dressed and made his way out to the living room. He stopped short seeing all of his gargoyle brethren sitting around waiting for him. "Um, hey guys, what's going on?"

Sebastian took charge. "Sit down." He pointed to the recliner which meant they would be sitting around him in a circle.

This cannot be good.

He had no choice, he sat down and tried to hide his hands at his side.

Sebastian shook his head at him. "Let me see them."

Toussaint was starting to panic. "You have this all wrong, Pascal and I must have been fooling around after we dropped Ivy off."

Pascal looked miserable, Toussaint knew what he was going to say. "After we dropped her off we went straight to bed. I made sure you were asleep before I went to my own room."

Asald leaned forward. "What about this morning? I found you at work, asked about your hands, and you took off. Hours later, we find you asleep in your room after being missing all day."

This statement shocked Toussaint, he had no memory of seeing Asald this morning or talking to him about his hands. And somehow, he had lost an entire day?

Sebastian was radiating authority, it was something Toussaint never expected to experience firsthand. "What did you do to Ivy to send her racing out of town? And don't even think about lying to me; I'm going to get in contact with her either way and make sure she's okay."

Toussaint shook his head as he stared around the room at his brother and his best friends. "You know I would never hurt anyone. Whatever it is, you think I did you're wrong."

He stood to walk out, hurt that after hundreds of years together they didn't believe him.

Sebastian grabbed something off the coffee table and thrust it in his face. It was an iPad with a video frozen on it. He didn't want to press play, scared to know what he was going to see.

Inpatient for Toussaint to comply, Sebastian reached up and pressed the button. Toussaint recognized it as the view outside of the police station, which just happened to be next to Saroj's. At first, there was nothing but an empty sidewalk, then there's an audible crunching noise as the giant ice cream cone was thrown on the ground. Toussaint had to swallow a mouth full of bile when he watched himself land next to it, pick it up and throw it through the window of the ice cream shop.

Shocked to his core, he fell back into the chair. How did he have no memory of doing this? Dread filled him if this were true, then he had to believe the flashes of memories with Ivy were too. He needed to save her.

"I'll go talk to Saroj now. I'll apologize for getting so drunk and promise to fix everything for free. I'll do the same with Alizon and Seren, I'll make everything better."

He stood to leave, but Sebastian grabbed his arm. "I don't think you should go anywhere right now."

Pascal cleared his throat. "Let him go Seb, he made a mistake; he needs to make it right."

Toussaint could tell Sebastian was fighting some internal struggle. Finally, he let Toussaint's arm go. "Let us know when you are going to start working on their stores, we'll help."

He nodded, then raced out of the apartment. He had every intention of rectifying the damage he did, but first, he needed to make a stop and see if he was losing his mind.

Thirty-One

Ivy's wrists were numb, she had been tied to the chair for hours. The sun was almost gone, and the worst part was she had no idea where Zeus was.

Toussaint had driven a little ways off the main road then left the car there. He wouldn't let her take the dog when he demanded they start walking. He cracked the windows and said he'd deal with him later.

Ivy assumed she knew what that meant and her heart was broken. Toussaint had kept a steel grip on her arm as he marched her through the woods. After what felt like a mile or longer walk, they came to a cabin. Ivy's heart sank seeing it looked completely abandoned.

She didn't resist when he took her inside, she was still trying to figure out what to do next. It wasn't until he pulled a pile of rope out of a closet that she tried to run. Toussaint laughed as he dragged her to a chair and tied her to it.

"Toussaint please, this isn't you, let me go."

The creature in front of her laughed as he grabbed a chair and sat across from her. As scared as she was, she still couldn't help studying the wings protruding from his back. Her mind wasn't accepting what she was seeing.

"You're right, this isn't Toussaint. He's in here but taking a little nap."

Ivy was stunned, but as long as he was talking, she was going to keep him occupied. "Who are you, and what do you want from me?"

His eyes sparkled with excitement. "I am no one of importance to you, and I could care less about you. However, I was summoned here, so I'm bound to complete my tasks before I can be released."

Ivy had more questions than answers, she started with the most obvious. "Who summoned you to do what tasks?"

"Let's just say this town has an infestation problem and I'm the exterminator. They don't want humans here, you were getting to cozy with this dolt, so I'm here to run you off. My summoner must be new, they didn't know they have to give extremely explicit instructions or my kind tend to stretch the boundaries." He stood up and grabbed a bottle of water out of a cabinet. "I was told to run you out of town. Here we are, *out of town*, I guess I did my job, and now I get to have a little fun. I'm going to give you some water now then I'm going to get food and come back here. I'm going to enjoy taking my time torturing you."

Ivy screamed, this time it was a blood curdling, bone-chilling scream. The creature rolled its eyes then knocked her upside the head making her lose consciousness.

It was almost night time, and he still hadn't returned. She tried to stay calm; eventually, someone at work would notice she had stopped working and would go looking for her. Penny would get nervous when Ivy didn't let her know she was home safe. Her situation sucked, but there was no reason to panic, yet.

The rope biting into her wrists were tearing more and more flesh the longer she struggled to get free. She knew she was bleeding; hopefully, it would make it easier for her to slide the rope off, so she fought through the pain and kept trying.

***

At some point in the night, Ivy had fallen asleep. Toussaint hadn't returned; she was starving, and she needed to go to the bathroom.

The next time she woke up, it was daylight again, and she felt weak. Maybe forcing herself to bleed had been a bad idea. It may be crazy, but right then she was praying her captor would come back.

At least she wouldn't be left here to die slowly.

Thirty-Two

Toussaint drove to Ivy's temporary apartment. He didn't see her car in the parking lot. He took the stairs two at a time and banged on the door. Desperate for confirmation he put his shoulder against it and forced it open.

As he feared, the place was empty. She had obviously left in a hurry, he called her cell phone again, but it went to voicemail.

He went back outside, trying to piece together the images in his mind. They were foggy as if they weren't his own.

Sebastian was leaning against his truck waiting for him. "Was she there?"

Toussaint hung his head in shame. "No, and don't ask me again what happened. I don't know."

"Aristide is going into the city first thing tomorrow to check on her. I don't believe you did anything to her, but I have to be sure she's okay."

"I appreciate that I really do."

Sebastian patted his shoulder, "how about we go talk to some upset store owners now? They're waiting for us at the station."

It was only two blocks away, so Toussaint chose to walk as slowly as he could, desperate to come up with the right thing to say to his friends.

Sebastian led him into the station and straight to his office where Saroj, Alizon, and Seren sat waiting.

Saroj hopped up and hugged Toussaint, it made him feel even worse. "I don't blame you, everyone gets drunk sometimes and in all my years knowing you I've never seen you out of control. We'll rebuild that ice cream cone bigger and better than before."

Toussaint was ashamed, he collapsed into the only other open chair. "I don't remember being that drunk or doing anything to your stores. I am truly sorry, I can't begin to explain why I did it."

Seren stood and walked towards him. "I'm not mad either. I did lose a lot of rare herbs and ingredients for my potions. I would appreciate the help restocking the store." He patted him on the shoulder and left the office.

Toussaint glanced up at Alizon, she sat there studying him quietly before sighing. "I don't know what we did to make you choose our stores, but I know you didn't do it on purpose. I've been thinking about remodeling anyways, maybe you gave me the push I needed." She walked over and kissed the top of his head. "Don't beat yourself up over this."

Toussaint wanted to cry, this was probably the worst thing he had ever done in his life and to friends no less, and they all forgave him.

Sebastian sat behind his desk. "You look like shit, go home and get some sleep. I'll let Pascal know you're on your way."

Toussaint understood the unstated message. He still didn't trust him and wanted him off the street.

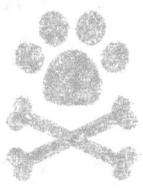

Thirty-Three

A sound outside the cabin door had Ivy's eyes fluttering open. Her eyes barely focused, it wasn't till he was standing in front of her that she could see it was Toussaint.

"Hey, you're still with me. I wanted to come back and play last night. The other bird brains in town were watching me a little too closely. I had to wait for his idiot brother to jump in the shower before sneaking out."

She didn't want to beg for anything but the bottle of water had been laying on the floor tormenting her for two almost two days. "Can I please have some water?" Her voice was scratchy, it burned her throat to talk.

He glanced around and found the bottle. "Oh yeah, I don't want you leaving me too soon.

What fun would that be?" He poured the liquid down her throat, she chugged until she coughed.

He sat in the chair across from her and pulled a knife out of his pocket. "I can hear his thoughts, you know. He's an absolute bore, he tortured himself trying to stay away from you. He would have done it too if you hadn't thrown yourself at him. He's never going to forgive himself for doing this to you." He walked up and slowly dragged the tip of the knife down her cheek, the scraping had her frozen in fear that he would push deeper. "I promise when this is all over I'll make sure he can remember everything I've done to you, so it torments him for the rest of his life."

Ivy wasn't able to be strong any longer, she whimpered, terror engulfing her. She had to fight back, she didn't want to be a meek victim that just let death come to her. "He'll always be a better man than you. You're so weak you can't even walk around as yourself, you have to be a part of him. Does it hurt knowing you need the big strong man in order for you to be here?"

The force of the slap stunned Ivy, her chair was thrown back, she hit her head on the floor and screamed his name before she lost consciousness again. Her last thought was relief that she at least wouldn't know when the end came.

"Ivy wake up, come on baby, open your eyes."

Her head was throbbing, she opened her eyes and found Toussaint leaning over her. She tried to scream, but he stood up and held his arms out. "Wait, it's me. I don't know what's happening or how we got here, but it's me. I heard you yell for me and suddenly I was here." He slowly bent down and cut the ropes from her arms.

She was too sore to move on her own. "I can't move, my muscles are stiff."

He scooped her up and set her on the chair he had vacated. "I can feel something inside of me, what's going on?"

She looked at him warily, it sounded like her Toussaint but what if he was toying with her.

He stroked the quickly growing lump on her cheek. "Tell me I didn't do this?"

She nodded. "There's some creature inside you, he's going to torture and kill me then let you take the blame for it."

She could see the shock in his eyes, he really had no idea. "Hang on."

She watched as he walked over to a cabinet and pulled out a handgun then grabbed bullets out of a drawer. "Tie me up then go get the guys. Leave the gun with me, now that I can feel it there I'll try to control it." He sat down and waited for her to grab the rope. "Leave the gun, if I feel him winning. I'll take myself out."

She backed away, refusing to touch the gun. "No, you aren't killing yourself."

"If it gets you again it won't hesitate to kill you, let me protect you."

Ivy didn't want to listen, but she had no other choice. She wasn't strong enough to fight him, and she wasn't even sure she had enough energy to find her way out of the woods.

She grabbed the rope and tied the knots the best she could. She cupped his cheeks and kissed him lightly. "We'll be back for you."

She grabbed the bottle of water and left. Looking in every direction there was nothing except forest, she had no idea which way to go. Walking quickly, she took off in the general direction she thought they had come from.

Everything looked the same, she had no idea where she was going. A gunshot in the distance made her jump, then the realization hit her. She crumpled to the ground sobbing, Toussaint had sacrificed himself for her.

She laid there crying, too tired to keep going. A flapping noise grew louder by the second, she looked up and saw Toussaint flying towards her. She tried to scurry backward. "No, no, no." There was no bullet wound, this was not her Toussaint.

She got up and ran, she knew there was no point, but she had to try. Seconds later, she heard the most glorious sound in the world.

She could hear Zeus barking, she glanced back and saw Toussaint turning away from her. He was retreating.

She ran a few more yards, following the sounds of Zeus's barking. She broke down in tears as Seraphine, Zeus, and all of Toussaint's friends came into view. Sebastian spotted her first and ran to catch her; now that she was safe, she didn't have any energy left to keep going.

Seraphine pushed through the guys and grabbed Ivy's hand. "It's Toussaint, isn't it?"

Ivy shook her head. "He's being possessed by something, he tried to fight it."

Seraphine turned to the rest of the group. "Find him and bring him to my house." Ivy stared in disbelief as Sebastian, Asald, Pascal, and Aristide stretched their backs, allowing large wings to unfold. They sprang into the air and took off. "Saroj, take Ivy and carry her to the car. I'll call Dr. Larson and King, and have them meet us."

Ivy had never been carried by anyone before, normally she would have been uncomfortable, but at that moment she was safe, and that's all that mattered. She curled against his chest and fell asleep, she'd had enough flying men for one day.

Thirty-Four

Toussaint jerked awake as his body was falling to the ground. Once the creature was able to take over and rip through the ropes, Toussaint had tried to fight. He knew Ivy wouldn't survive if he let the creature win. He had the gun to his head and was about to pull the trigger when his head jerked back. The beast didn't want him dying, with a final surge of energy it took control and Toussaint was pushed into the background, forced to watch but unable to get control back.

He hated being trapped inside his own head. At least he was able to know what was going on and try to help. When the creature found Ivy in the woods, he tried to scream. It didn't do any good.

An icy shaft of fear ran through him as the creature caught sight of the rescue group coming after him. Toussaint didn't care if they hurt him, he just wanted Ivy safe.

It turned and fled, thinking it could outfly the other four gargoyles. At some point, it must have realized it didn't have a shot. It released it's hold on him, he got back control seconds before he smashed onto the forest floor.

He laid there, relieved that Ivy was safe, pissed that he let himself be controlled, in pain from the fall and ashamed to face his friends when they caught up to him.

It didn't take long before he saw Pascal and the others hovering above him. "It's okay, it's me. I'm not going to resist."

They cautiously swooped down and surrounded him.

"Whatever has been messing with me took off as soon as it saw you guys."

Sebastian crossed his arms. "How do we know you aren't the creature and your lying to us?"

Toussaint didn't have a good response, he didn't know something had been inside him so how should they know.

Pascal held a hand out to help him up. "Seraphine will know."

The group took off into the air, Toussaint's bodyguards staying close to him on all sides. They flew straight to Seraphine's, he followed Sebastian as he landed in the back garden and walked him through the back of the house.

Part of him wanted to see Ivy and make sure she was okay, the other part of him was too ashamed to see her.

Seraphine stood outside of a large, intricately carved wooden door. "King's inside, let's get started."

Nausea washed over Toussaint. King was the owner of Hell's Brew coffee shop in town, but more importantly, he was one of the Princes of Hell. Toussaint always tried to keep his distance from him. Not that King was a bad guy, more because gargoyles are susceptible to demonic possession, so he figured why tempt fate.

That last thought was a lightbulb going off in his head. The creature must have been a demon, now the question was why King summoned him there. Toussaint marched into the room, he wanted answers.

The dark and brooding man leaned against a wall across the room. He looked relaxed, but Toussaint knew it was all an act. "Have a seat, let's see what's going on with you."

Seraphine grabbed Toussaint's elbow and pulled him over to a chair in the center of the room. He glanced around, there were candles lit throughout the room, the walls were stone, and there was a large altar table on a dais near where King stood.

Toussaint did as instructed and sat, he was relieved they didn't make him lay on the table like an animal waiting for sacrifice.

King walked over and leaned down to look in his eyes. The whites of his eyes disappeared, they were a black pool of nothingness. He chuckled and stood back up. "Ajax, what are you doing?"

Everyone in the room glanced around, trying to figure out who he was talking to. He ignored the questioning looks and focused on Toussaint.

"You know the pain I can inflict on you, don't bother hiding, let's talk."

Toussaint gasped as he felt the creature still inside him. He thought he'd left, instead, he hid like a coward. Before he could say anything, Ajax took back control.

"Raguel, sire, I meant no offense -"

King shook his head at him cutting him off. "You know not to come here, especially without being summoned."

The creature forced Toussaint's body to jump out of the chair and kneel at King's feet. "I beg you to believe me, I was summoned here, I thought by you. When I got here, I was immediately bound by someone. She gave me instructions, I couldn't resist, or her spell was set to incinerate me."

Seraphine stepped forward and kneeled next to him. "Who was she? What did she want you to do?"

The creature continued to grovel at his master's feet. "She wants all humans gone from here; I was supposed to get rid of the girl and make it look like she left of her own free will."

King toed him with his boot, "Who was she?"

"I can't - "He gasped in pain, Toussaint felt like every cell of his body was on fire "- I'm bound to keep her secret. If I tell, her spell will kill me."

The Prince grabbed him around the neck and threw him back into the chair. "Tell me her name or I will kill you."

The more the creature tried to do as his master demanded, the more the pain grew. Together he and the creature screamed, begging for the torture to end.

Ajax finally gave in. "Her name was...." One last scream before the fire overtook them, the taste of smoke the last thing Toussaint knew before death came.

Thirty-Five

Ivy's eyes fluttered open. She was in a bedroom, Zeus was lying next to her, and an IV was sticking in her arm. A man she didn't know walked over and sat on the edge of the bed. "How are you feeling?"

She took stock of her body before responding. "Tired and hungry." She glanced around and noticed the room was empty except for them. "Where is everyone?"

Saroj came through the door. "He just got here, he's going to see King now."

Ivy assumed the *he* they were talking about was Toussaint but she didn't know what King was.

Saroj walked over and leaned down to pat her hand. "I'm glad you're awake. I was worried about you. Dr. Larson here is the best in town, well his twin might argue that."

Ivy turned to study the other man. "Sarah mentioned Dr. Larson took care of her last year."

"That would be the brother Saroj mentioned, we run the clinic in town."

She nodded and turned back to Saroj. "Is Toussaint alright?"

Saroj nodded, "He looked okay when I saw them take him into the room."

"Who is King?"

The two men exchanged glances. "I'll send Seraphine in to talk to you in a little bit. For now, you should rest. You lost a lot of blood, and you are seriously dehydrated."

Ivy closed her eyes to do as she was told when screaming reverberated through the house. The lights flickered on and off a few times. She knew what that was, something happened to Toussaint. She got up to go find him when a piercing scream exploded through the room seconds before the lights went out completely.

She cried out, scared that meant Toussaint was gone. Saroj rubbed her arm as she sobbed. The door to the bedroom opened, Seraphine waved Dr. Larson over. He left the room, and Seraphine came in and sat on the edge of the bed.

"I'm sure you have questions."

Ivy thought that was the understatement of the year. Should she start with the flying men or the guy that glowed silver?

Seraphine saved her the trouble. "Black Hollow is a town of paranormals. Some people like Sarah and Silver are human, almost everyone else is not."

Ivy glanced up at Saroj but didn't say anything.

Seraphine chuckled. "Saroj is a Yeti. He knows ice better than anyone. Toussaint, Pascal, Sebastian, Asald, and Aristide are all gargoyles."

Ivy gasped, she had no idea Asald wasn't human. He was odd, but she never would have guessed he had wings and could fly. "What about Adam and Derrick? They both seemed different."

"Adam is Frankenstein's monster; the scars are from him being put together. Derrick is a zombie..." Ivy subconsciously grabbed her blanket and pulled it tight as if that was going to help. "Not like a flesh-eating zombie, that's a myth. In truth, most of what you know about paranormals is probably wrong. I know this is shocking, so take your time."

Ivy shook her head, "Actually I thought I was starting to lose my mind, everything makes so much more sense now. I assume dragons and shifters are real based off some of the signs that were made at the shower?"

Seraphine laughed, "Yes, we have many of those and so much more. We keep to ourselves here and don't invite outsiders in. Most of us have come here for refuge from the outside world that would try to destroy us if they knew the truth. I hope we can count on you to keep our secret?"

Ivy didn't have a chance to answer, Penny came running into the room, the door banging against the wall. She launched herself into Ivy and hugged her. "What is with this town and hurting humans."

Seraphine stood up. "That's a great question and one we are a little closer to figuring out."

Sebastian walked in and came over to Ivy. "I'm sorry I let this happen. I knew something was off with Toussaint, I should have watched him better. Do you want to press charges against him?"

Ivy gasped and shook her head vehemently. "No, he tried to shoot himself for me. I know that wasn't him hurting me."

"You're a better person than I am," Penny mumbled.

Ivy looked between Seraphine and Sebastian. "So, does that mean he's okay? I heard the screams."

Sebastian nodded. "He's unconscious but alive. When King tried to get the name of the person responsible, the demon was killed trying to obey. We've never had anything like this happen. Toussaint's body is alive, we have to assume he's inside there too."

Ivy's heart sank, this was all her fault. If she hadn't pushed him so hard, she wouldn't have gotten a target drawn on their backs. She should have just done the wedding and left. Because of her, he was in a coma.

Epilogue

Two weeks later

Ivy closed the lid of her laptop and stretched her back. Thank god her work was flexible. It had been two weeks since she was taken hostage. She didn't feel right leaving with Toussaint unconscious, so she stayed in town.

During the day she sat at his place and watched over him while she worked. At night she hung out with the various residents of town getting to know them and their true identities. Everyone had been so sweet to her, she couldn't imagine any of them had tried to intentionally hurt her or any other human.

Both Dr. Larson's came by regularly to check on Toussaint. They couldn't explain why he was still unconscious. The mysterious King who turned out to be a freaking Prince of Hell said he still sensed Toussaint's soul so Ivy held out hope that he was just taking a nap and would come back to them soon.

Right on time, Pascal came home, like every other day they would wash Toussaint then she would leave him to watch over his brother for the night.

He kicked his shoes off and grabbed a beer out of the fridge. "How's our patient today?"

"No change, I thought I saw his hand move once. After a good twenty minutes of staring and waiting for it to happen again, I gave up. I'll let Dr. Larson know just in case when they come by tomorrow.

She filled a bucket with soapy water and grabbed washcloths. Pascal followed her into Toussaint's room and helped roll him onto his side so she could wash his back. It still amazed her that there were wings under his skin; she had spent hours studying his shoulders, and she couldn't find any indication of where they came out.

Pascal rolled him back down, she reached down and pulled one leg out from under the sheet.

"I really hope you are going to wash the rest of what's under the sheet and not my brother?"

Ivy screamed, Pascal jumped, and Toussaint laughed.

Tears burned her eyes. "Oh, thank god, you're okay."

Pascal grabbed his brother and pulled him into a hug. "Don't you ever leave me again."

Ivy's heart melted seeing the tears roll down Pascal's cheeks. He had been so strong over the last couple of weeks, she really wasn't sure how affected he was until now.

He set him back down slowly then left the room, Ivy assumed he needed a minute to compose himself.

She grabbed Toussaint's hand and squeezed. "You had us so scared."

"Should I assume by the sponge bath that I've been out for a bit?"

She nodded, "It's been just over two weeks."

Toussaint's jaw dropped, she would be shocked too if it was her.

He studied her face for a second, "I am so sorry I hurt you. Why are you still here? You should have run for the hills as soon as you were rescued."

Ivy shook her head, "I know it wasn't you, you didn't hurt me."

"I wasn't strong enough to protect you either."

She leaned down so her face was inches from his. "You did something better, you were willing to kill yourself so I could get away. If you wanted me to love you, you could have just taken me on a few dates, you didn't need to risk sacrificing love to prove a point."

The End

Keep reading for a sneak peak of the next book in the Black Hollow series *Scaling His Heart* by Sheri Lyn releases August 5th, 2019.

Scaling His Heart

Coming August 5th, 2019

Tristan yawned as he finished the paperwork for another successful night of cooking at the Scales and Tails restaurant. It wasn't what he thought he'd be doing with his life, but he couldn't deny it wasn't fulfilling, albeit a tad lonely at times. When you lived as long as his kind did, things began to get monotonous after the first few centuries.

"Tristan?" Nerissa called out as she came into his office. "You almost done? I'm ready to get out of here."

"Hell yes. Just finished actually. I've got a list of what you need to order on the next supply shipment. Inventory is such a pain in the ass to do. Now let's get out of here. I'm dying to go for a swim to wash the days dust off." Tristan stood and stretched with a smile. "How'd I do, boss lady?"

Nerissa rolled her eyes, "I'm not your boss, and you know damn well you kick ass in the kitchen. For us being a simple fish and chips place, we're getting a reputation for some amazing and unique dishes."

They'd just stepped out the back door and were locking it when Tristan heard Seraphine's voice call out for him. He froze, glanced to Nerissa and whimpered. "Did she say my name?"

"Yes, sorry brother, but I'm out of here. You're on your own." Nerissa winked, waved to Seraphine and was gone from sight in a matter of seconds.

"Hi, Seraphine." Tristan turned and tried to smile but he wasn't sure if it was more of a grimace or not.

Seraphine laughed before taking his arm, "Walk with an old lady, won't you."

"You're sprier than half the citizens in this town. Don't play me." Tristan scoffed as he began to relax as they walked. "Where are we headed?"

"You're going home, right? I'll walk with you and we can talk."

Tristan nodded, but as the minutes passed and she didn't say anything the more his fear was building. Everyone knew if Seraphine came around, she was up to something or new something that would affect you in some way. The only question that remained was if it was good or bad.

"We're going to have a new resident of Black Hollow soon. He's making his way here slowly as he's had to come a long way. I don't know much about him yet, but he's a water dweller. I am hoping that you and your sister would be kind enough to let him stay in one of your spare rooms until we can get him permanently settled someplace."

"Oh, yes of course we can do that. I've got a wing to myself, there's plenty of room for him to stay as long as needed. And of course, we have a rather large lake he can use. As a matter of fact, I surprised Nerissa a few hundred birthdays back with a remodel that gave both wings direct access to the lake from inside. Our new resident will love it."

Tristan knew he was babbling but he was nervous. It wasn't often the town matriarch came to you and said house a stranger. But he trusted her, if she said to do this, he would. She always knew what was best for the town and the residents.

"That's great. I'm sure it's been a welcome addition for you both and our new guest will love it as well. He should be arriving some time in the next hour or so. If you don't mind I'll bring him over as soon as he does."

"Sure, we'll be up. We might go for a swim, but I'll have Ollie stay close to the surface and watch for you guys. He'll find us within seconds and we can be up to meet you."

Seraphine smiled, "I haven't seen Ollie in ages. I miss that little guy. How's my favorite otter doing anyway?"

"He's good, feisty as usual. Loves to torment Cuddles, which drives Nerissa insane. That of course, in turn, makes me very happy."

She laughed, "Typical siblings. Go on with you now. I'll see you in a bit. Enjoy your swim."

Tristan watched her walk away until the darkness quickly hid her from his view. Nerissa wasn't going to be happy, but it wasn't like they had much choice. He just didn't want to hear her bitching about sharing the house. Hence why he'd offered his wing of the house. She wouldn't have to run into the stranger unless she ventured out of her wing.

The smartest thing they'd ever done was build this house like they had. Each side was self-sustaining, without the need to come out if they didn't choose too. There were common areas in the middle of course, but now that it was only the two of them, they didn't use it much. They saw each other all the time while working. At home, they needed the break.

"So?" Nerissa called as he approached the front door to their house.

"New resident needs a place, he needs to be near water. He's going to stay on my side until they figure something else out. I don't know anything about him other than that, so don't ask. And don't bitch, you know you'd have said yes if she'd come to you instead of me."

Nerissa frowned but agreed. "You're right. I'm just cranky, I want to swim, I'm feeling dried out, my body is screaming for the comforting water to engulf me."

"Me too, give me two minutes and I'll meet you in the water. Have you seen Ollie? I need to talk to him."

"Yup, he's mad you left him at home today, so be prepared to suck up."

Tristan groaned, "Guess it's a good thing I brought home a bribe, even though I made him stay home for punishment."

They parted ways and headed to their rooms. Tristan called out to Ollie with pips, pops, and squeaks, but the little shit refused to reply. "Come on, after all these years, you think I don't know you can understand me."

All of a sudden, a small bundle raced at him and climbed up to sit on his shoulder as he chittered and squeaked back at him in anger.

"No, I don't feel bad. You destroyed my favorite shell bracelet, and don't even try that. There was no food inside. I've had it for years. You were just mad."

Ollie chittered once more, sat back and waited. Tristan tried to hide his smile at his obstinate friend. "It just so happens that I need a favor, I'll give you the treat I brought even though your apology was half-assed."

He cocked his head, before nodding making Tristan laugh as he pulled the small fishes from his pocket. "You can have these, but I need you to stay close and watch for Seraphine. When she gets here, come find us right away. Deal?"

Ollie stared at the fish, narrowed his eyes and then looked back to Tristan and squealed with a nod of his small head.

"Good, get down and I'll give it to you. You're not eating on my shoulder ever again. You make a mess and the smell is impossible to get out of my clothes."

***

"Nerissa, Ollie just told me our new guest is onshore with Seraphine. I'm heading back. You coming with?"

"Yup, right behind you. I'm curious and want to know more. Mainly what he is that he needs water."

Tristan climbed out of the lake and made the short walk back to his bedroom. He quickly threw on some clothes and headed downstairs where Ollie told him they were waiting.

"There you are, I hope I gave you enough time to enjoy your swim?" Seraphine called out as soon as she saw him coming down the stairs.

"It was good, I could have stayed for a few more hours, but it's not like I can't go..." He trailed off as he caught sight of the stranger sitting on the couch a few feet away. He was gorgeous, chiseled, lean and the epitome of tall dark and fuckable.

"Lachlan Muir I'd like you to meet your new roommate, Tristan Falkenberg. Tristan this is Lachlan, he came all the way from Scotland to find a safe place to live." Seraphine smiled and clapped her hands. "You two get to know each other. If you need anything you know how to find me."

Tristan gaped as he watched Seraphine turn and disappear. "Uh hi, Lachlan." He mumbled as he felt his face flush in embarrassment. "Welcome to Black Hollow."

The Black Hollow Series

The town of Black Hollow has many more stories to tell. Please visit the website and join the Facebook group to know when the next story is releasing.

https://www.blackhollowtown.com/

https://www.facebook.com/blackhollowtown/

Books in the Black Hollow Series
(In order by Publication Date)

Loving the Monster Within (Prequel)

by Cassidy K. O'Connor

Reviving Love by Cassidy K. O'Connor

Silver Linings by Sheri Lyn

Finding Her Fire by Gracen Miller

One Man's Curse by Jennifer Wedmore

It's the Little Things by Robbie Cox

Resurrecting His Heart by J.C. Layne

~Other Books by the Author~

ABOUT THE AUTHOR

Cassidy lives in the Tampa, Florida area with her high school sweetheart, their three children, two crazy dogs, a guinea pig and a skinny pig. She loves reading and going to the movies but not nearly as much as she enjoys watching her kids either playing ball or performing with one of their instruments. She also loves to travel and hopes to one day watch a baseball game in every MLB stadium in the country.

To learn more about Cassidy please visit her online at www.cassidykoconnor.com.

You can also find her on Facebook at www.facebook.com/cassidykoconnorauthor

She always welcomes new friends and encourages readers to reach out to her.